Leigh Hunt

An answer to the question 'what is poetry?'

Including remarks on versification

Leigh Hunt

An answer to the question 'what is poetry?'
Including remarks on versification

ISBN/EAN: 9783337111472

Printed in Europe, USA, Canada, Australia, Japan

Cover: Foto ©Andreas Hilbeck / pixelio.de

More available books at **www.hansebooks.com**

Leigh Hunt

AN ANSWER TO THE QUESTION

'WHAT IS POETRY?'

INCLUDING

REMARKS ON VERSIFICATION

EDITED BY

ALBERT S. COOK

PROFESSOR OF THE ENGLISH LANGUAGE AND LITERATURE
IN YALE UNIVERSITY

GINN AND COMPANY

BOSTON · NEW YORK · CHICAGO · LONDON

The Athenæum Press

GINN AND COMPANY · PRO-
PRIETORS · BOSTON · U.S.A.

PREFACE.

Tnr essay here reprinted is the initial one in
Leigh Hunt's *Imagination and Fancy*, which is
among the very best of his prose works. In the
Preface to that volume, which was published in
1844, he thus describes his object in writing it :
"to furnish such an account, in an Essay, of the
nature and requirements of poetry, *as may enable
readers in general to give an answer on those points
to themselves and others.*" The whole volume is
suggestive, so much so that Ruskin refers to it as
an "admirable piece of criticism," and adds that it
"ought to be read with care" (*Modern Painters*,
Vol. III., 'Of Imagination Penetrative'). Still,
the opening essay is the only part of the book
which bears the character of sustained exposition,
the remainder consisting mostly of poetical extracts,
with brief introductions and comments ; it is, accord-
ingly the part which is likely to prove most accept-
able to students of the theory and art of poetry.

The author is frequently inaccurate in quotation ;
as there is no advantage, but rather loss, in perpet-

uating the results of inadvertence, I have endeavored to verify all the passages cited, and to conform them to the reading of the most authoritative editions. In the cases where I have not succeeded, I shall be grateful for information from those who are better read. With reference to the use of italics for emphasis, in which Hunt abounds, I need scarcely say that I have made no change.

As Leigh Hunt gave to the volume from which this essay is taken the title of *Imagination and Fancy*, and as he has much to say on these two subjects, it has seemed to me that students might be glad of the opportunity to consult with ease the principal discussions of these two related faculties, antecedent to the date of Hunt's volume. I have therefore collected in a note near the end of this book the chief passages from Coleridge and Wordsworth bearing upon this subject, together with those from Jean Paul upon which Coleridge is supposed to have built his theory.

ALBERT S. COOK.

YALE UNIVERSITY, Feb. 27, 1893.

WHAT IS POETRY?

INCLUDING

REMARKS ON VERSIFICATION.

POETRY, strictly and artistically so called, that is to say, considered not merely as poetic feeling, which is more or less shared by all the world, but as the operation of that feeling, such as we see it in the poet's book,[1] is the utterance of a 5 passion for truth, beauty, and power, embodying and illustrating its conceptions by imagination and fancy, and modulating its language on the principle of variety in uniformity. Its means are whatever the universe contains ; and its ends, 10 pleasure and exaltation. Poetry stands between nature and convention, keeping alive among us the enjoyment of the external and the spiritual world ; it has constituted the most enduring fame of nations ; and, next to Love and Beauty, which 15 are its parents, is the greatest proof to man of the pleasure to be found in all things, and of the probable riches of infinitude.

Poetry is a passion,[1] because it seeks the deepest impressions; and because it must undergo, in order to convey them.

It is a passion for truth, because without truth the impression would be false or defective.

It is a passion for beauty, because its office is to exalt and refine by means of pleasure, and because beauty is nothing but the loveliest form of pleasure.

It is a passion for power, because power is impression triumphant, whether over the poet, as desired by himself, or over the reader, as affected by the poet.

It embodies and illustrates its impressions by imagination, or images of the objects of which it treats, and other images brought in to throw light on those objects, in order that it may enjoy and impart the feeling of their truth in its utmost conviction and affluence.

It illustrates them by fancy, which is a lighter play of imagination, or the feeling of analogy coming short of seriousness, in order that it may laugh with what it loves, and show how it can decorate it with fairy ornament.

It modulates what it utters, because in running the whole round of beauty it must needs include beauty of sound; and because, in the height of

[1] *Passio*, suffering in a good sense, — ardent subjection of one's self to emotion.   (Author's note.)

its enjoyment, it must show the perfection of its triumph, and make difficulty itself become part of its facility and joy.

And lastly, Poetry shapes this modulation into uniformity for its outline, and variety for its parts, because it thus realizes the last idea of beauty itself, which includes the charm of diversity within the flowing round of habit and ease.

Poetry is imaginative passion. The quickest and subtlest test of the possession of its essence is in expression; the variety of things to be expressed shows the amount of its resources; and the continuity of the song completes the evidence of its strength and greatness. He who has thought, feeling, expression, imagination, action, character, and continuity, all in the largest amount and highest degree, is the greatest poet.

Poetry includes whatsoever of painting can be made visible to the mind's eye,[1] and whatsoever of music can be conveyed by sound and proportion without singing or instrumentation. But it far surpasses those divine arts in suggestiveness, range, and intellectual wealth;—the first, in expression of thought, combination of images, and the triumph over space and time; the second, in all that can be done by speech, apart from the tones and modulations of pure sound. Painting and music, however, include all those portions of the gift of poetry that can be expressed and heightened by the visible and melodious. Paint-

---

[1] But see the arguments in Lessing's *Laokoon*.

ing, in a certain apparent manner, is things themselves ; music, in a certain audible manner, is
their very emotion and grace. ` Music and paint-
ing are proud to be related to poetry, and poetry
5 loves and is proud of them.

Poetry begins where matter of fact or of science
ceases to be merely such, and to exhibit a further
truth, that is to say, the connection it has with
the world of emotion, and its power to produce
10 imaginative pleasure. Inquiring of a gardener,
for instance, what flower it is we see yonder, he
answers, 'A lily.' This is matter of fact. The
botanist pronounces it to be of the order of
'Hexandria monogynia.'[1]   This is matter of
15 science. It is the 'lady' of the garden,[2] says
Spenser ; and here we begin to have a poetical
sense of its fairness and grace.   It is

> The plant and flower of *light*,

says Ben Jonson ;[3] and poetry then shows us the
20 beauty of the flower in all its mystery and
splendor.

If it be asked, how we know perceptions like
these to be true, the answer is, by the fact of
their existence — by the consent and delight of
25 poetic readers.   And as feeling is the earliest
teacher, and perception the only final proof of
things the most demonstrable by science, so the
remotest imaginations of the poets may often be

---

[1] In the Linnæan system.
[2] Rather of the 'flowering field.' See *F. Q.* 2. 6. 16.
[3] In the *Pindaric Ode on the Death of Sir H. Morison.*

found to have the closest connection with matter
of fact ; perhaps might always be so, if the subtlety
of our perceptions were a match for the causes of
them.   Consider this image of Ben Jonson's — of
a lily being the flower of light.   Light, undecom-   5
posed, is white ; and as the lily is white, and
light is white, and whiteness itself is nothing *but*
light, the two things, so far, are not merely
similar, but identical.   A poet might add, by
an analogy drawn from the connection of light   10
and color, that there is a 'golden dawn' issuing
out of the white lily, in the rich yellow of the
stamens.   I have no desire to push this similarity
farther than it may be worth.   Enough has been
stated to show that, in poetical as well as in   15
other analogies, 'the same feet of Nature,' as
Bacon says, may be seen 'treading in different
paths';[1] and that the most scornful, that is to
say, dullest disciple of fact, should be cautious
how he betrays the shallowness of his philosophy   20
by discerning no poetry in its depths.

   But the poet is far from dealing only with these
subtle and analogical truths.   Truth of every kind
belongs to him, provided it can bud into any kind
of beauty, or is capable of being illustrated and   25
impressed by the poetic faculty.   Nay, the sim-

---

[1] From the *Advancement of Learning* 2. 5. 3: 'Neither are
these only similitudes, as men of narrow observation may
conceive them to be, but the same footsteps treading or printing
upon several subjects or matters.' Also in *De Augment Scient.*
cap. 1. lib. iii. (ed. of Spedding, Ellis, and Heath, 1. 543).   The
hint was probably taken from Shelley's *Defense of Poetry*, 5 4.

plest truth is often so beautiful and impressive of itself, that one of the greatest proofs of his genius consists in his leaving it to stand alone, illustrated by nothing but the light of its own tears or smiles, its own wonder, might, or playfulness.   Hence the complete effect of many a simple passage in our old English ballads and romances, and of the passionate sincerity in general of the greatest early poets, such as Homer and Chaucer, who flourished before the existence of a 'literary world,' and were not perplexed by a heap of notions and opinions, or by doubts how emotion ought to be expressed.   The greatest of their successors never write equally to the purpose, except when they can dismiss everything from their minds but the like simple truth.   In the beautiful poem of Sir Eger, Sir Graham, and Sir Gray-Steel (see it in Ellis's Specimens, or Laing's Early Metrical Tales [1]), a knight thinks himself disgraced in the eyes of his mistress : —

> Sir Eger says,[2] 'If it be so,
> Then wot I well I must forgo
> Love-liking, and manhood, all clean.'
> *The water rushed out of his een!*

Sir Gray-Steel is killed : —

> Gray-Steel into his death thus thrawes [throes ?]
> He *walters* [welters, — throws himself about] *and*
> *the grass up drawes;*

> *   *   *   *   *

---

[1] Lines 773 - 776.   A different version may be found in *Bishop Percy's Folio Manuscript* I. 341. 100.

[2] Hunt, 'said.'

A little while then lay he still,
(Friends that him saw liked full ill)
And blood[1] into his armour bright.[2]

The abode of Chaucer's Reve, or Steward, in the Canterbury Tales, is painted in two lines 5 which nobody ever wished longer : —

His wonyng [dwelling] was ful fair upon an heeth ;
With grene trees i-shadwed was his place.[3]

Every one knows the words of Lear, 'most *matter-of-fact*, most melancholy ' : [4] —   10

Pray, do not mock me :
I am a very foolish fond old man,
Fourscore and upward, not an hour more nor less ;
And, to deal plainly,
I fear I am not in my perfect mind.[5]   15

It is thus, by exquisite pertinence, melody, and the implied power of writing with exuberance, if need be, that beauty and truth become identical in poetry, and that pleasure, or at the very worst, a balm in our tears, is drawn out of pain.   20

It is a great and rare thing, and shows a lovely imagination, when the poet can write a commentary, as it were, of his own, on such sufficing passages of nature, and be thanked for the addition. There is an instance of this kind in Warner, an 25

[1] So Laing; Ellis and Hunt have 'bled.'
[2] Lines 1611-1612, 1615-1617.
[3] *Prologue* 606-607.
[4] Adapted from Milton's *Il Penseroso* 62: 'Most musical, most melancholy.'
[5] *King Lear* 4. 7. 59-63.

old Elizabethan poet, than which I know nothing
sweeter in the world.   He is speaking of Fair
Rosamond, and of a blow given her by Queen
Eleanor : —

5 With that she dasht her on the lippes, *so dyèd double red :
Hard was the heart that gave the blow, soft were those
lips that bled.*[1]

There are different kinds and degrees of imagination, some of them necessary to the formation
10 of every true poet, and all of them possessed by
the greatest.   Perhaps they may be enumerated
as follows : — First, that which presents to the
mind any object or circumstance in every-day life ;
as when we imagine a man holding a sword, or
15 looking out of a window ; — Second, that which
presents real, but not every-day circumstances ;
as King Alfred tending the loaves,[2] or Sir Philip
Sidney giving up the water to the dying soldier ;
— Third, that which combines character and
20 events directly imitated from real life, with imita-
tive realities of its own invention ; as the probable
parts of the histories of Priam and Macbeth, or
what may be called natural fiction as distinguished
from supernatural ; — Fourth, that which conjures
25 up things and events not to be found in nature ;
as Homer's gods and Shakespeare's witches,

[1] *Albion's England* 8. 41. 53; ed. of 1597, p. 201.   Modern
editions usually print as four lines, and so Hunt did; it is here
changed to conform to the original.
[2] See Pauli's *Alfred the Great* (Bohn series), p. 101.

enchanted horses and spears,[1] Ariosto's hippogriff,[2] &c.; — Fifth, that which, in order to illustrate or aggravate one image, introduces another :)
sometimes in simile, as when Homer compares
Apollo descending in his wrath at noon-day to the   5
coming of night-time;[3] sometimes in metaphor,
or simile comprised in a word, as in Milton's
'motes that *people* the sunbeams';[4] sometimes
in concentrating into a word the main history of
any person or thing, past or even future, as in the 10
'starry Galileo'[5] of Byron, and that ghastly fore-
gone conclusion of the epithet 'murdered' applied
to the yet living victim in Keats's story from
Boccaccio, —

> So the two brothers and their *murdered* man   15
> Rode past[6] fair Florence ;[7]—

sometimes in the attribution of a certain repre-
sentative quality which makes one circumstance
stand for others, as in Milton's gray-fly winding
its '*sultry* horn,'[8] which epithet contains the heat 20
of a summer's day ; — Sixth, that which reverses
this process, and makes a variety of circumstances
take color from one, like nature seen with jaun-
diced or glad eyes, or under the influence of storm

---

[1] See Chaucer, *Clerke's Tale;* Ariosto, *Orl. Fur.* 8. 17, etc.;
Spenser, *F. Q.* 3. 3. 60, etc. ; and especially Warton, *Hist.
Eng. Poetry* 2. 338 – 348, quoted in Skeat's edition of *The
Prioresses Tale*, etc., pp. xxxiii - xli.

[2] See p. 18.
[3] *Il.* 1. 47.
[4] *Il Pens.* 8.
[5] *Childe Harold* canto 4, st. 54.
[6] Hunt, 'towards.'
[7] *Isabella* st. 27.
[8] *Lyc.* 28.

or sunshine ; as when in Lycidas, or the Greek
pastoral poets, the flowers and the flocks are made
to sympathize with a man's death ;[1] or, in the
Italian poet, the river flowing by the sleeping
Angelica seems talking of love —

> Parea che l' erba a lei fiorisse intorno,
> *E d' amor ragionasse quella riva !*[2]—

or in the voluptuous homage paid to the sleeping
Imogen by the very light in the chamber and the
reaction of her own beauty upon itself ;[3] or in
the 'witch element' of the tragedy of Macbeth
and the May-day night[4] of Faust ; — Seventh, and
last, that which by a single expression, apparently
of the vaguest kind, not only meets but surpasses
in its effect the extremest force of the most
particular description ; as in that exquisite passage of Coleridge's Christabel, where the unsus-
pecting object of the witch's malignity is bidden
to go to bed : —

> Quoth Christabel, So let it be !
> And as the lady bade, did she.
> Her gentle limbs did she undress,
> *And lay down in her loveliness :*[5]—

a perfect verse surely, both for feeling and music.
The very smoothness and gentleness of the limbs
is in the series of the letter *l*'s.

[1] Ruskin's 'pathetic fallacy'; *Mod. Painters*, Part 4, Chap. 12.
[2] *Orl. Inn.* 1. 3. 69; Hunt inserts after the quotation, '*Orlando Innamorato*, canto iii.,' and writes 'le' for 'a lei.'
[3] *Cymbeline* 2. 2. 19 ff.
[4] Usually called the *Walpurgis Night's Dream.*
[5] Near the end of *Part the First.*

I am aware of nothing of the kind surpassing
that most lovely inclusion of physical beauty in
moral, neither can I call to mind any instances of
the imagination that turns accompaniments into
accessories, superior to those I have alluded to. 5
Of the class of comparison, one of the most
touching (many a tear must it have drawn from
parents and lovers) is in a stanza which has been
copied into the Friar of Orders Gray[1] out of
Beaumont and Fletcher :[2] — 10

> Weep no more, lady, weep no more,
>   Thy sorrow is in vaine ;
> *For violets pluckt the sweetest showers*
>   *Will ne'er make grow againe.*

And Shakespeare and Milton abound in the very 15
grandest ; such as Antony's likening his changing
fortunes to the cloud-rack ;[3] Lear's appeal to the
old age of the heavens ;[4] Satan's appearance in

[1] A cento composed by Bishop Percy out of fragments of the
old poets, and printed in the earlier editions of the *Reliques*.

[2] The stanza probably by Fletcher (Fleay thinks Field), who
may have been assisted in the composition of the play, *The
Queen of Corinth*, by others, or another, but hardly by Beaumont
(see Ward's *Eng. Dram. Lit.* 2. 220; *Englische Studien* 7. 75; 9.
22; 10. 390; Fleay, *Chronicle of the English Drama* 1. 206).
The stanza, which was not in the first edition, runs (*Q. C.* 3. 2.
1 – 4):
>   Weep no more, nor sigh, nor groan,
>   Sorrow calls no time that's gone;
>   Violets plucked, the sweetest rain
>   Makes not fresh nor grow again.

[3] *Ant. and Cl.* 4. 14. 3 – 14.
[4] *King Lear* 2. 4. 192 – 195.

the horizon, like a fleet 'hanging in the clouds;[1] and the comparisons of him with the comet[2] and the eclipse.[3]   Nor unworthy of this glorious company, for its extraordinary combination of delicacy and vastness, is that enchanting one of Shelley's in the Adonais : —

> Life, like a dome of many-colored glass,
> Stains the white radiance of eternity.[4]

I multiply these particulars in order to impress upon the reader's mind the great importance of imagination in all its phases, as a constituent part of the highest poetic faculty.

The happiest instance I remember of imaginative metaphor is Shakespeare's moonlight 'sleeping' on a bank ;[5] but half his poetry may be said to be made up of it, metaphor indeed being the common coin of discourse.   Of imaginary creatures none, out of the pale of mythology and the East, are equal, perhaps, in point of invention, to Shakespeare's Ariel and Caliban ; though poetry may grudge to prose the discovery of a Winged Woman, especially such as she has been described by her inventor in the story of Peter Wilkins ;[6] and in point of treatment, the Mam-

---

[1] *P. L.* 2. 637.

[2] *P. L.* 2. 708–716.

[3] *P. L.* 1. 576–579.

[4] Stanza 52. See W. M. Rossetti's note in his edition.

[5] *Merch. Ven.* 5. 1. 54.

[6] See the extract in Chambers' *Cycl. Eng. Lit.*   The novel is by R. Paltock (pub. 1757); a facsimile reprint has been edited by A. H. Bullen (London, 1884).

mon[1] and Jealousy[2] of Spenser, some of the
monsters in Dante, particularly his Nimrod,[3] his
interchangements of creatures into one another,
and (if I am not presumptuous in anticipating
what I think will be the verdict of posterity) the 5
Witch in Coleridge's Christabel, may rank even
with the creations of Shakespeare. It may be
doubted, indeed, whether Shakespeare had bile
and nightmare enough in him to have thought of
such detestable horrors as those of the interchang- 10
ing adversaries (now serpent, now man[4]), or even
of the huge, half-blockish enormity of Nimrod, —
in Scripture, the 'mighty hunter' and builder of
the tower of Babel,[5] — in Dante, a tower of a man
in his own person, standing with some of his 15
brother giants up to the middle in a pit in hell,
blowing a horn to which a thunder-clap is a
whisper, and hallooing after Dante and his guide
in the jargon of a lost tongue! The transfor-
mations are too odious to quote ; but of the 20
towering giant we cannot refuse ourselves the
'fearful joy' of a specimen. It was twilight,
Dante tells us, and he and his guide Virgil were
silently pacing through one of the dreariest regions
of hell, when the sound of a tremendous horn made 25
him turn all his attention to the spot from which
it came. He there discovered, through the dusk,
what seemed to be the towers of a city. Those
are no towers, said his guide ; they are giants,

[1] *F. Q.* Bk. 2, canto 7.
[2] *F. Q.* 3. 10. 52–60.
[3] See pp. 14–16.
[4] *Inferno*, canto 25.
[5] Gen. 10. 9, 10.

standing up to the middle in one of these circular
pits : —

> Come quando la nebbia si dissipa,
>   Lo sguardo a poco a poco raffigura
> 5   Ciò che cela il vapor, che l' aere stipa;
> Così forando l' aura grossa e scura,
>   Più e più appressando in vêr la sponda,
>   Fuggémi errore, e giungémi[1] paura:
> Pero chè come in su la cerchia tonda
> 10   Montereggion di torri si corona;
>   Così la proda, che il pozzo circonda,
> Torreggiavan di mezza la persona
>   Gli orribili giganti, cui minaccia
>   Giove del cielo ancora quando tuona.
> 15 Ed io scorgeva già d' alcun la faccia,
>   Le spalle, e il petto, e del ventre gran parte,
>   E per le coste giù ambo le braccia.
>
>   *   *   *   *
>
> La faccia sua mi parea lunga e grossa,
>   Come la pina di San Pietro a Roma;
> 20   E a sua proporzione eran l' altre ossa.
>
>   *   *   *   *
>
> 'Rafel mai amech zabi almi!'
>   Cominciò a gridar la fiera bocca,
>   Cui non si convenían più dolci salmi.
> E il duca mio vêr lui: 'Anima sciocca!
> 25   Tienti col corno, e con quel ti disfoga,
>   Quand' ira o altra passion ti tocca.
> Cercati al collo, e troverai la soga
>   Che il tien legato, o anima confusa,
>   E vedi lui che il gran petto ti doga.'
> 30 Poi disse a me: 'Egli stesso s' accusa:
>   Questi è Nembrotto, per lo cui mal coto
>   Pure un linguaggio nel mondo non s' usa.

---

[1] Scartazzini and some others prefer 'crescémi.'

Lasciamlo stare, e non parliamo a voto;
    Chè così è a lui ciascun linguaggio,
    Come il suo ad altrui, che a nullo è noto.'[1]

I looked again: and as the eye makes out,
By little and little, what the mist concealed,   5
In which, till clearing up, the sky was steeped;
So, looming through the gross and darksome air,
As we drew nigh, those mighty bulks grew plain,
And error quitted me, and terror joined:
For in like manner as all round its height   10
Montereggione crowns itself with towers,
So towered above the circuit of that pit,
Though but half out of it, and half within,
The horrible giants that fought Jove, and still
Are threatened when he thunders. As we neared   15
The foremost, I discerned his mighty face,
His shoulders, breast, and more than half his trunk,
With both the arms down hanging by the sides.
His face appeared to me, in length and breadth,
Huge as St. Peter's pinnacle at Rome,   20
And of a like proportion all his bones.
He opened, as we went, his dreadful mouth,
Fit for no sweeter psalmody: and shouted
After us, in the words of some strange tongue,
'Ràfel ma-èe amech zabèe almee!—'   25
'Dull wretch!' my leader cried, 'keep to thine horn,
And so vent better whatsoever rage
Or other passion stuff thee. Feel thy throat
And find the chain upon thee, thou confusion!
Lo! what a hoop is clenched about thy gorge.'   30
Then turning to myself, he said, 'His howl
Is its own mockery. This is Nimrod, he
Through whose ill thought it was that humankind

---

[1] *Inf.* 31. 34–81. Hunt inserts the reference after the quotation.

Were tongue-confounded.   Pass him, and say naught:
For as he speaketh language known of none,
So none can speak save jargon to himself.'[1]

Assuredly it could not have been easy to find a
fiction so uncouthly terrible as this in the hypo-
chondria of Hamlet.   Even his father had
evidently seen no such ghost in the other world.
All his phantoms were in the world he had left.
Timon, Lear, Richard, Brutus, Prospero, Macbeth
himself, none of Shakespeare's men had, in fact,
any thought but of the earth they lived on, whatever supernatural fancy crossed them.   The thing
fancied was still a thing of this world, 'in its
habit as it lived,'[2] or no remoter acquaintance
15 than a witch or a fairy.   Its lowest depths (unless
Dante suggested them) were the cellars under the
stage.   Caliban himself is a cross-breed between
a witch and a clown.   No offence to Shakespeare;
who was not bound to be the greatest of healthy
20 poets, and to have every morbid inspiration
besides.   What he might have done, had he set
his wits to compete with Dante, I know not; all
I know is, that in the infernal line he did nothing
like him; and it is not to be wished he had.   It
25 is far better that, as a higher, more universal, and
more beneficent variety of the genus Poet, he
should have been the happier man he was, and
left us the plump cheeks on his monument,
instead of the carking visage of the great, but
30 over-serious, and comparatively one-sided Floren-

---

[1] Cf. the prose translation by Norton.   [2] *Haml.* 3. 4. 135.

tine. Even the imagination of Spenser, whom
we take to have been a 'nervous gentleman' compared with Shakespeare, was visited with no such
dreams as Dante. Or, if it was, he did not choose
to make himself thinner (as Dante says *he* did) 5
with dwelling upon them. He had twenty visions
of nymphs and bowers, to one of the mud of Tar-
tarus.[1] Chaucer, for all he was 'a man of this
world' as well as the poets' world, and as great,
perhaps a greater enemy of oppression than 10
Dante, besides being one of the profoundest masters of pathos that ever lived, had not the heart
to conclude the story of the famished father and
his children, as finished by the inexorable anti-
Pisan.[2] But enough of Dante in this place. 15
Hobbes, in order to daunt the reader from objecting to his friend Davenant's want of invention,
says of these fabulous creations in general, in his
letter prefixed to the poem of Gondibert, that
'impenetrable armors, enchanted castles, invul- 20
nerable bodies, iron men, flying horses, and a
thousand other such things, [which][3] are easily
feigned by them that dare.' These are girds at
Spenser and Ariosto. But, with leave of Hobbes
(who translated Homer as if on purpose to show 25
what execrable verses could be written by a phi-
losopher), enchanted castles and flying horses are
not easily feigned, as Ariosto and Spenser feigned
them; and that just makes all the difference.
For proof, see the accounts of Spenser's en- 30

---

[1] Cf. *F. Q.* 1. 5. 33.   [2] *Inf.* 33. 1–90; *Monk's Tale.*
[3] Hunt omits 'which.'

chanted castle in Book the Third, Canto Twelfth,
of the Fairy Queen; and let the reader of Italian
open the Orlando Furioso at its first introduction
of the Hippogriff,[1] where Bradamante, coming to
5 an inn, hears a great noise, and sees all the people
looking up at something in the air; upon which,
looking up herself, she sees a knight in shining
armor riding towards the sunset upon a creature
with variegated wings, and then dipping and dis-
10 appearing among the hills.[2]   Chaucer's steed of
brass, that was

> So horsly and so quik of ye,[3]

is copied from the life.   You might pat him and
feel his brazen muscles.   Hobbes, in objecting to
15 what he thought childish, made a childish mistake.
His criticism is just such as a boy might pique
himself upon, who was educated on mechanical
principles, and thought he had outgrown his
Goody Two-shoes.   With a wonderful dimness of
20 discernment in poetic matters, considering his
acuteness in others, he fancies he has settled the
question by pronouncing such creations 'impossible!'   To the brazier they are impossible, no

[1] l. 4. Hunt introduces the reference, parenthetically, into
the text, but wrongly, as 3. 4.

[2] The prototype of the Hippogriff is Pegasus, for which see
Hawthorne's *Tanglewood Tales*, The Chimæra.   The earliest
mention of Pegasus is in Hesiod.   Chaucer recognizes the likeness of his horse of brass to Pegasus (*Clerk's Tale* 207–208):

> And seyden, it was lyk the Pegasee,
> The hors that hadde winges for to flee.

[3] *Squire's Tale* 194.

doubt; but not to the poet. Their possibility, if the poet wills it, is to be conceded; the problem is, the creature being given, how to square its actions with probability, according to the nature assumed of it. Hobbes did not see that the skill [5] and beauty of these fictions lay in bringing them within those very regions of truth and likelihood in which he thought they could not exist. Hence the serpent Python of Chaucer,

Slepynge agayn [1] *the sonne upon a day.* [2] [10]

when Apollo slew him. Hence the chariot-drawing dolphins [3] of Spenser, softly swimming along the shore lest they should hurt themselves against the stones and gravel. Hence Shakespeare's Ariel, living under blossoms, and riding at even- [15] ing on the bat; and his domestic namesake [4] in the Rape of the Lock (the imagination of the drawing-room) saving a lady's petticoat from the coffee with his plumes, and directing atoms of snuff into a coxcomb's nose. In the Orlando [20] Furioso [5] is a wild story of a cannibal necromancer, who laughs at being cut to pieces, coming together again like quicksilver, and picking up his head when it is cut off, sometimes by the hair, sometimes by the nose! This, which would [25] be purely childish and ridiculous in the hands of an inferior poet, becomes interesting, nay grand,

[1] Hunt, 'against.'
[2] *Manciple's Tale* 6.
[3] *F. Q.* 3. 4. 33, 34.
[4] Not he, but his legions; see 3. 115; 5. 83.
[5] 15. 65. Hunt introduces the reference in parenthesis.

in Ariosto's, from the beauties of his style, and its
conditional truth to nature.   The monster has a
fated hair on his head—a single hair[1]—which
must be taken from it before he can be killed.
5 Decapitation itself is of no consequence, without
that proviso.   The Paladin Astolfo, who has
fought this phenomenon on horseback, and succeeded in getting the head and galloping off with
it, is therefore still at a loss what to be at.   How
10 is he to discover such a needle in such a bottle of
hay?   The trunk is spurring after him to recover
it, and he seeks for some evidence of the hair in
vain.   At length he bethinks him of scalping the
head.   He does so; and the moment the opera-
15 tion arrives at the place of the hair, *the face of the
head becomes pale, the eyes turn in their sockets,*
and the lifeless pursuer tumbles from his horse:

> Si fece il viso allor pallido e brutto,
> Travolse gli occhi, e dimostrò all' occaso
> 20 Per manifesti segni esser condutto:
> E 'l busto che seguia troncato al collo,
> Di sella cadde, e diè l' ultimo crollo.[2]

> Then grew the visage pale, and deadly wet,
> The eyes turned in their sockets, drearily:
> 25 And all things show'd the villain's sun was set.
> His trunk that was in chase, fell from its horse,
> And, giving the last shudder, was a corse.

It is thus, and thus only, by making Nature his
companion wherever he goes, even in the most

---

[1] Apparently a reminiscence of Virgil. *Georg.* 1. 404 ff.; Ovid,
Metamorph. 8. 1 ff.; or the pseudo-Virgilian *Ciris.*
[2] *Orl. Fur.* 15. 87.

supernatural region, that the poet, in the words
of a very instructive phrase, takes the world along
with him.   It is true, he must not (as the Plato-
nists would say) humanize weakly or mistakenly
in that region; otherwise he runs the chance of   5
forgetting to be true to the supernatural itself,
and so betraying a want of imagination from that
quarter.   His nymphs will have no taste of their
woods and waters; his gods and goddesses be
only so many fair or frowning ladies and gentle-   10
men, such as we see in ordinary paintings; he will
be in no danger of having his angels likened to a
sort of wild-fowl, as Rembrandt has made them in
his Jacob's Dream.   His Bacchuses will never
remind us, like Titian's, of the force and fury, as   15
well as of the graces of wine.   His Jupiter will
reduce no females to ashes; his fairies be nothing
fantastical; his gnomes, not 'of the earth,
earthy.'[1]   And this again will be wanting to
Nature; for it will be wanting to the super-   20
natural, as Nature would have made it, working in
a supernatural direction.   Nevertheless, the poet,
even for imagination's sake, must not become a
bigot to imaginative truth, dragging it down into
the region of the mechanical and the limited, and   20
losing sight of its paramount privilege, which is
to make beauty, in a human sense, the lady and
queen of the universe.   He would gain nothing
by making his ocean-nymphs mere fishy creatures,
upon the plea that such only could live in the

[1] 1 Cor. 15. 47.

water; his wood-nymphs with faces of knotted oak; his angels without breath and song, because no lungs could exist between the earth's atmosphere and the empyrean. The Grecian tendency in this respect is safer than the Gothic; nay, more imaginative; for it enables us to imagine *beyond* imagination, and to bring all things healthily round to their only present final ground of sympathy — the human. When we go to heaven, we may idealize in a superhuman mode, and have altogether different notions of the beautiful; but till then we must be content with the loveliest capabilities of earth. The sea-nymphs of Greece were still beautiful women, though they lived in the water. The gills and fins of the ocean's natural inhabitants were confined to their lowest semi-human attendants; or if Triton himself was not quite human, it was because he represented the fiercer part of the vitality of the seas, as they did the fairer.

To conclude this part of my subject, I will quote from the greatest of all narrative writers two passages; — one exemplifying the imagination which brings supernatural things to bear on earthly, without confounding them; the other that which paints events and circumstances after real life. The first is where Achilles, who has long absented himself from the conflict between his countrymen and the Trojans, has had a message from heaven bidding him reappear in the enemy's sight, standing outside the camp-wall upon the trench, but doing nothing more; that is to say, taking no part in the fight. He is simply to be seen. The two armies down by the sea-side are contending which shall possess the body of Patroclus; and the mere sight of the 5 dreadful Grecian chief — supernaturally indeed impressed upon them, in order that nothing may be wanting to the full effect of his courage and conduct upon courageous men — is to determine the question. We are to imagine a slope of 10 ground towards the sea, in order to elevate the trench; the camp is solitary; the battle ('a dreadful roar of men,' as Homer calls it) is raging on the sea-shore; and the goddess Iris has just delivered her message and disappeared:— 15

Αὐτὰρ Ἀχιλλεὺς ὧρτο διίφιλος· ἀμφὶ δ' Ἀθήνη
Ὤμοις ἰφθίμοισι βάλ' αἰγίδα θυσσανόεσσαν·
Ἀμφὶ δέ οἱ κεφαλῇ νέφος ἔστεφε δῖα θεάων
Χρύσεον, ἐκ δ' αὐτοῦ δαῖε φλόγα παμφανόωσαν.
Ὡς δ' ὅτε καπνὸς ἰὼν ἐξ ἄστεος αἰθέρ' ἵκηται   20
Τηλόθεν ἐκ νήσου, τὴν δήϊοι ἀμφιμάχωνται·
Οἵ τε πανημέριοι στυγερῷ κρίνονται Ἄρηϊ
Ἄστεος ἐκ σφετέρου· ἅμα δ' ἠελίῳ καταδύντι
Πυρσοί τε φλεγέθουσιν ἐπήτριμοι, ὑψόσε δ' αὐγὴ
Γίγνεται ἀΐσσουσα, περικτιόνεσσιν ἰδέσθαι,   25
Αἵ κέν πως σὺν νηυσὶν ἄρης ἀλκτῆρες ἵκωνται·
Ὡς ἀπ' Ἀχιλλῆος κεφαλῆς σέλας αἰθέρ' ἵκανεν.

Στῆ δ' ἐπὶ τάφρον ἰὼν ἀπὸ τείχεος· οὐδ' ἐς Ἀχαιοὺς
Μίσγετο· μητρὸς γάρ πυκινὴν ὠπίζετ' ἐφετμήν.
Ἔνθα στὰς ἤϋσ'· ἀπάτερθε δὲ Παλλὰς Ἀθήνη   30
Φθέγξατ'· ἀτὰρ Τρώεσσιν ἐν ἄσπετον ὦρσε κυδοιμόν.

'Ως δ' ὅτ' ἀριζήλη φωνή, ὅτε τ' ἴαχε σάλπιγξ
Ἄστυ περιπλομένων δηΐων ὑπὸ θυμοραϊστέων·
Ὥς τότ' ἀριζήλη φωνὴ γένετ' Αἰακίδαο.
Οἱ δ' ὡς οὖν ἄϊον ὄπα χάλκεον Αἰακίδαο.
5 Πᾶσιν ὀρίνθη θυμός· ἀτὰρ καλλίτριχες ἵπποι
Ἄψ ὄχεα τρόπεον· ὄσσοντο γὰρ ἄλγεα θυμῷ.
Ἡνίοχοι δ' ἔκπληγεν, ἐπεὶ ἴδον ἀκάματον πῦρ
Δεινὸν ὑπὲρ κεφαλῆς μεγαθύμου Πηλείωνος
Δαιόμενον· τὸ δὲ δαῖε θεὰ γλαυκῶπις Ἀθήνη.
10 Τρὶς μὲν ὑπὲρ τάφρου μεγάλ' ἴαχε δῖος Ἀχιλλεύς,
Τρὶς δ' ἐκυκήθησαν Τρῶες κλειτοί τ' ἐπίκουροι.
Ἔνθα δὲ καὶ τότ' ὄλοντο δυώδεκα φῶτες ἄριστοι
Ἀμφὶ σφοῖς ὀχέεσσι καὶ ἔγχεσιν.[1]

But up Achilles rose, the loved of heaven;
15 And Pallas on his mighty shoulders cast
The shield of Jove; and round about his head
She put the glory of a golden mist,
From which there burnt a fiery-flaming light.
And as, when smoke goes heavenward from a town,
20 In some far island which its foes besiege,
Who all day long with dreadful martialness
Have poured from their own town: soon as the sun
Has set, thick lifted fires are visible,
Which, rushing upward, make a light in the sky,
25 And let the neighbors know, who may perhaps
Bring help across the sea; so from the head
Of great Achilles went up an effulgence.

Upon the trench he stood, without the wall,
But mixed not with the Greeks, for he revered
30 His mother's word: and so, thus standing there,
He shouted: and Minerva, to his shout,
Added a dreadful cry; and there arose
Among the Trojans an unspeakable tumult.

---

[1] *Il.* 18. 203-231. Hunt introduces the reference into the text.

And as the clear voice of a trumpet, blown
Against the town by spirit-withering foes,
So sprang the clear voice of Æacides.
And when they heard the brazen cry, their hearts
All leaped within them; and the proud-maned horses 5
Ran with the chariots round, for they foresaw
Calamity; and the charioteers were smitten,
When they beheld the ever-active fire
Upon the dreadful head of the great-minded one
Burning; for bright-eyed Pallas made it burn. 10
Thrice o'er the trench divine Achilles shouted;
And thrice the Trojans and their great allies
Rolled back: and twelve of all their noblest men
Then perished, crushed by their own arms and chariots.

Of course there is no further question about the 15
body of Patroclus. It is drawn out of the press,
and received by the awful hero with tears.

The other passage is where Priam, kneeling
before Achilles, and imploring him to give up the
dead body of Hector, reminds him of his own 20
father; who, whatever (says the poor old king)
may be his troubles with his enemies, has the
blessing of knowing that his son is still alive, and
may daily hope to see him return. Achilles, in
accordance with the strength and noble honesty 25
of the passions in those times, weeps aloud himself at this appeal, feeling, says Homer, 'desire'
for his father in his very 'limbs.'[1] He joins in
grief for the venerable sufferer, and can no longer
withstand the look of his 'gray head and his gray 30
chin.' Observe the exquisite introduction of this
last word. It paints the touching fact of the
chin's being imploringly thrown upward by the

[1] But this line (514) is generally regarded as spurious.

kneeling old man, and the very motion of his
beard as he speaks:—

Ὣς ἄρα φωνήσας ἀπέβη πρὸς μακρὸν Ὄλυμπον
Ἑρμείας· Πρίαμος δ' ἐξ ἵππων ἆλτο χαμᾶζε,
5   Ἰδαῖον δὲ κατ' αὖθι λίπεν· ὁ δὲ μίμνεν ἐρύκων
Ἵππους ἡμιόνους τε· γέρων δ' ἰθὺς κίεν οἴκου,
Τῇ ῥ' Ἀχιλεὺς ἵζεσκε, διίφιλος· ἐν δέ μιν αὐτὸν
Εὗρ'. ἕταροι δ' ἀπάνευθε καθείατο· τῷ δὲ δύ' οἴω
Ἥρως Αὐτομέδων τε, καὶ Ἄλκιμος ὄζος Ἄρηος,
10 Ποίπνυον παρεόντε· νέον δ' ἀπέληγεν ἐδωδῆς.
Ἔσθων καὶ πίνων, ἔτι καὶ παρέκειτο τράπεζα·
Τοὺς δ' ἔλαθ' εἰσελθὼν Πρίαμος μέγας, ἄγχι δ' ἄρα στὰς,
Χερσὶν Ἀχιλλῆος λάβε γούνατα, καὶ κύσε χεῖρας
Δεινὰς, ἀνδροφόνους, αἵ οἱ πολέας κτάνον υἶας.
15 Ὡς δ' ὅτ' ἂν ἄνδρ' ἄτη πυκινὴ λάβῃ, ὅστ'. ἐνὶ πάτρῃ
Φῶτα κατακτείνας, ἄλλον ἐξίκετο δῆμον,
Ἀνδρὸς ἐς ἀφνειοῦ, θάμβος δ' ἔχει εἰσορόωντας·
Ὡς Ἀχιλεὺς θάμβησεν, ἰδὼν Πρίαμον θεοειδέα·
Θάμβησαν δὲ καὶ ἄλλοι, ἐς ἀλλήλους δὲ ἴδοντο.
20 Τὸν καὶ λισσόμενος Πρίαμος πρὸς μῦθον ἔειπεν.

Μνῆσαι πατρὸς σοῖο, θεοῖς ἐπιείκελ' Ἀχιλλεῦ,
Τηλίκου, ὥσπερ ἐγών, ὀλοῷ ἐπὶ γήραος οὐδῷ.
Καὶ μέν που κεῖνον περιναιέται ἀμφὶς ἐόντες
Τείρουσ', οὐδέ τις ἐστίν, ἀρὴν καὶ λοιγὸν ἀμῦναι·
25 Ἀλλ' ἦ τοι κεῖνός γε, σέθεν ζώοντος ἀκούων,
Χαίρει τ' ἐν θυμῷ, ἐπί τ' ἔλπεται ἤματα πάντα
Ὄψεσθαι φίλον υἱὸν, ἀπὸ Τροίηθεν ἰόντα·
Αὐτὰρ ἐγὼ πανάποτμος, ἐπεὶ τέκον υἶας ἀρίστους
Τροίῃ ἐν εὐρείῃ, τῶν δ' οὔ τινά φημι λελεῖφθαι.
30 Πεντήκοντά μοι ἦσαν, ὅτ' ἤλυθον υἷες Ἀχαιῶν·
Ἐννεακαίδεκα μέν μοι ἰῆς ἐκ νηδύος ἦσαν,
Τοὺς δ' ἄλλους μοι ἔτικτον ἐνὶ μεγάροισι γυναῖκες.
Τῶν μὲν πολλῶν θοῦρος Ἄρης ὑπὸ γούνατ' ἔλυσεν·
Ὃς δέ μοι οἶος ἔην, εἴρυτο δὲ ἄστυ καὶ αὐτούς,

Τὸν σὺ πρώην κτεῖνας, ἀμυνόμενον περὶ πάτρης,
Ἕκτορα· τοῦ νῦν εἵνεχ᾽ ἱκάνω νῆας Ἀχαιῶν,
Λυσόμενος παρὰ σεῖο, φέρω δ᾽ ἀπερείσι᾽ ἄποινα.
Ἀλλ᾽ αἰδεῖο θεοὺς, Ἀχιλεῦ, αὐτόν τ᾽ ἐλέησον,
Μνησάμενος σοῦ πατρός· ἐγὼ δ᾽ ἐλεεινότερός περ,   5
Ἔτλην δ᾽, οἳ οὔπω τις ἐπιχθόνιος βροτὸς ἄλλος,
Ἀνδρὸς παιδοφόνοιο ποτὶ στόμα χεῖρ᾽ ὀρέγεσθαι.
Ὣς φάτο· τῷ δ᾽ ἄρα πατρὸς ὑφ᾽ ἵμερον ὦρσε γόοιο.
Ἀψάμενος δ᾽ ἄρα χειρὸς, ἀπώσατο ἦκα γέροντα.
Τὼ δὲ μνησαμένω, ὁ μὲν Ἕκτορος ἀνδροφόνοιο,   10
Κλαῖ᾽ ἀδινά, προπάροιθε ποδῶν Ἀχιλῆος ἐλυσθείς·
Αὐτὰρ Ἀχιλλεὺς κλαῖεν ἑὸν πατέρ᾽, ἄλλοτε δ᾽ αὖτε
Πάτροκλον· τῶν δὲ στοναχὴ κατὰ δώματ᾽ ὀρώρει.
Αὐτὰρ, ἐπεὶ ῥα γόοιο τετάρπετο δῖος Ἀχιλλεύς,
[Καί οἱ ἀπὸ πραπίδων ἦλθ᾽ ἵμερος, ἠδ᾽ ἀπὸ γυίων.]   15
Αὐτίκ᾽ ἀπὸ θρόνου ὦρτο, γέροντα δὲ χειρὸς ἀνίστη.
Οἰκτείρων πολιόν τε κάρη, πολιόν τε γένειον.[1]

So saying, Mercury vanished up to heaven;
And Priam then alighted from his chariot,
Leaving Idæus with it, who remained   20
Holding the mules and horses; and the old man
Went straight indoors, where the beloved of Jove
Achilles sat, and found him.   In the room
Were others, but apart; and two alone,
The hero Automedon, and Alcimus,   25
A branch of Mars, stood by him.   They had been
At meals, and had not yet removed the board.
Great Priam came, without their seeing him,
And kneeling down, he clasped Achilles' knees,
And kissed those terrible, homicidal hands,   30
Which had deprived him of so many sons,
And as a man who is pressed heavily
For having slain another, flies away
To foreign lands, and comes into the house

[1] *Il.* 24. 468–516.   As in 24, note.

Of some great man, and is beheld with wonder,
So did Achilles wonder to see Priam;
And the rest wondered, looking at each other.
But Priam, praying to him, spoke these words:—
5 'God-like Achilles, think of thine own father!
To the same age have we both come, the same
Weak pass: and though the neighboring chiefs may vex
Him also, and his borders find no help,
Yet when he hears that thou art still alive,
10 He gladdens inwardly, and daily hopes
To see his dear son coming back from Troy.
But I, bereaved old Priam! I had once
Brave sons in Troy, and now I cannot say
That one is left me.   Fifty children had I,
15 When the Greeks came, nineteen were of one womb;
The rest my women bore me in my house.
The knees of many of these fierce Mars has loosened;
And he who had no peer, Troy's prop and theirs,
Him hast thou killed now, fighting for his country,
20 Hector; and for his sake am I come here
To ransom him, bringing a countless ransom.
But thou, Achilles, fear the gods, and think
Of thine own father, and have mercy on me:
For I am much more wretched, and have borne
25 What never mortal bore, I think, on earth,
To lift unto my lips the hand of him
Who slew my boys.'

                    He ceased; and there arose
Sharp longing in Achilles for his father:
30 And taking Priam by the hand, he gently
Put him away; for both shed tears to think
Of other times; the one, most bitter ones
For Hector, and with wilful wretchedness
Lay right before Achilles: and the other,
35 For his own father now, and now his friend,
And the whole house might hear them as they moaned.

But when divine Achilles had refreshed
His soul with tears, and sharp desire had left
His heart and limbs, he got up from his throne,
And raised the old man by the hand, and took
Pity on his gray head and his gray chin.   5

O lovely and immortal privilege of genius! that
can stretch its hand out of the wastes of time,
thousands of years back, and touch our eyelids
with tears. In these passages there is not a word
which a man of the most matter-of-fact understand- 10
ing might not have written, *if he had thought of
it.* But in poetry, feeling and imagination are
necessary to the perception and presentation even
of matters of fact. They, and they only, see what
is proper to be told, and what to be kept back; 15
what is pertinent, affecting, and essential. Without feeling, there is a want of delicacy and distinction; without imagination there is no true
embodiment. In poets, even good of their kind,
but without a genius for narration, the action 20
would have been encumbered or diverted with ingenious mistakes. The over-contemplative would
have given us too many remarks; the over-lyrical,
a style too much carried away; the over-fanciful,
conceits and too many similes; the unimagina- 25
tive, the facts without the feeling, and not even
those. We should have been told nothing of
the 'gray chin,' of the house hearing them as
they moaned, or of Achilles gently putting the
old man aside; much less of that yearning for his 30
father, which made the hero tremble in every limb.

Writers without the greatest passion and power
do not feel in this way, nor are capable of expressing the feeling; though there is enough sensibility and imagination all over the world to enable
5 mankind to be moved by it, when the poet strikes
his truth into their hearts.

The reverse of imagination is exhibited in pure
absence of ideas, in commonplaces, and, above
all, in conventional metaphor, or such images and
10 their phraseology as have become the common
property of discourse and writing.   Addison's
Cato is full of them: —

> Passion unpitied and successless love
> *Plant daggers in my heart.*[1]

15
> I've sounded my Numidians, man by man,
> And find 'em *ripe for a revolt.*[2]

> The virtuous Marcia *towers above her sex.*[3]

Of the same kind is his 'courting the yoke' —
'distracting my very soul'[4] — 'calling up all'
20 one's 'father' in one's soul — 'working every
nerve' — 'copying a bright example;'[5] in short
the whole play, relieved now and then with a
smart sentence or turn of words.   The following
is a pregnant example of plagiarism and weak
25 writing.   It is from another tragedy of Addison's
time, — the Mariamne of Fenton: —

---

[1] 1. 1.   Hunt has 'breast' for 'heart.'   [2] 1. 3.

[3] 1. 4.   [4] Hunt writes 'heart.'   [5] All from 1. 1.

Marianne, *with superior charms,*
Triumphs o'er reason; in her look she *bears*
A paradise of ever-blooming sweets;
Fair as the first idea beauty *prints*
In the young lover's soul; a winning grace   5
Guides every gesture, and obsequious love
Attends on all her steps.

'Triumphing o'er reason' is an old acquaintance of everybody's. 'Paradise in her look' is from the Italian poets through Dryden. 'Fair as the first 10 idea,' &c., is from Milton,[1] spoilt; 'winning grace' and 'steps' from Milton[2] and Tibullus,[3] both spoilt. Whenever beauties are stolen by such a writer, they are sure to be spoilt; just as when a great writer borrows, he improves. 15

To come now to Fancy, — she is a younger sister of Imagination, without the other's weight of thought and feeling. Imagination indeed, purely so called, is all feeling; the feeling of the subtlest and most affecting analogies; the percep- 20 tion of sympathies in the natures of things, or in their popular attributes. Fancy is a sporting with their resemblance, real or supposed, and with airy and fantastical creations: —

— Rouse yourself; and the weak wanton Cupid   25
Shall from your neck unloose his amorous fold,
And, like a dew-drop from the lion's mane,
Be shook to air.[4]

---

[1] *P. L.* 7. 557.
[2] *P. L.* 8. 61, 489.
[3] *Tibullus* 4. 2. 7–8.
[4] *Troilus and Cressida* 3. 3. 222–225. As in 24, note.

That is imagination; — the strong mind sympathizing with the strong beast, and the weak love
identified with the weak dew-drop.

> And I, forsooth, in love! I, that have been love's whip;
> 5   *A very beadle to a humorous sigh;*
> A domineering pedant o'er the boy;
>
> *   *   *   *   *   * [1]
>
> This whimpled, whining, purblind, wayward boy;
> This senior-junior, giant-dwarf, Dan Cupid;
> *Regent of love-rimes, lord of folded arms,*
> 10   *The anointed sovereign of sighs and groans,* &c.[2]

That is fancy; — a combination of images not in
their nature connected, or brought together by
the feeling, but by the will and pleasure; and
having just enough hold of analogy to betray it
15 into the hands of its smiling subjector.

> Silent icicles
> *Quietly shining to the quiet moon.*[3]

That, again, is imagination — analogical sympathy;
and exquisite of its kind it is.

> 20   You are now sailed *into the north of my lady's opinion;*
> where you will hang *like an icicle on a Dutchman's beard,*
> unless you do redeem it by some laudable attempt.[4]

And that is fancy; — one image capriciously suggested by another, and but half connected with
25 the subject of discourse; nay, half opposed to

---

[1] One line omitted, but no break indicated by Hunt.

[2] *Love's Labor's Lost* 3. 1. 176–184. As in 24, note. Hunt
introduces the quotation with an ‘Oh!’ which is not in Shakespeare.

[3] Coleridge's *Frost at Midnight.* As in 24, note.

[4] *Twelfth Night* 3. 2. 28–31. As in 24, note.

it; for in the gaiety of the speaker's animal
spirits, the 'Dutchman's beard' is made to repre-
sent the lady!

Imagination belongs to Tragedy, or the serious
muse; Fancy to the comic. Macbeth, Lear, 5
Paradise Lost, the poem of Dante, are full of
imagination: the Midsummer Night's Dream and
the Rape of the Lock, of fancy; Romeo and
Juliet, the Tempest, the Fairy Queen, and the
Orlando Furioso, of both. The terms were 10
formerly identical, or used as such; and neither
is the best that might be found. The term
Imagination is too confined; often too material.
It presents too invariably the idea of a solid
body — of 'images' in the sense of the plaster- 15
cast cry about the streets. Fancy, on the other
hand, while it means nothing but a spiritual
image or apparition (φάντασμα. appearance,
phantom), has rarely that freedom from visibility
which is one of the highest privileges of imagina- 20
tion. Viola, in Twelfth Night, speaking of some
beautiful music, says: —

> It gives a very echo to the seat
> Where Love is throned.[1]

In this charming thought, fancy and imagination 25
are combined; yet the fancy, the assumption of
Love's sitting on a throne, is the image of a solid
body; while the imagination, the sense of sympathy between the passion of love and impassioned music, presents us no image at all. Some 30

[1] 2. 4. 21–22.

new term is wanting to express the more spiritual sympathies of what is called Imagination.

One of the teachers of Imagination is Melancholy; and like Melancholy, as Albert Dürer has painted her, she looks out among the stars, and is busied with spiritual affinities and the mysteries of the universe. Fancy turns her sister's wizard instruments into toys. She takes a telescope in her hand, and puts a mimic star on her forehead, and sallies forth as an emblem of astronomy. Her tendency is to the childlike and sportive. She chases butterflies, while her sister takes flight with angels. She is the genius of fairies, of gallantries, of fashions; of whatever is quaint and light, showy and capricious; of the poetical part of wit. She adds wings and feelings to the images of wit; and delights as much to people nature with smiling ideal sympathies, as wit does to bring antipathies together, and make them strike light on absurdity. Fancy, however, is not incapable of sympathy with Imagination. She is often found in her company; always, in the case of the greatest poets; often in that of less, though with them she is the greater favorite. Spenser has great imagination and fancy too, but more of the latter; Milton both also, the very greatest, but with imagination predominant; Chaucer the strongest imagination of real life, beyond any writers but Homer, Dante, and Shakespeare, and in comic painting inferior to none; Pope has hardly any imagination, but he has a great deal f-fancy; Coleridge little fancy, but imagination xquisite.   Shakespeare alone, of all poets that ver lived, enjoyed the regard of both in equal erfection.   A whole fairy poem of his writing vill be found in the present volume.[1]   See also is famous description of Queen Mab and her quipage, in Romeo and Juliet:[2]—

> Her wagon-spokes made of long spinners' legs,
> The cover of the wings of grasshoppers,
> The[3] traces of the smallest spider's web,
> The collars of the moonshine's watery beams, &c.

That is Fancy, in its playful creativeness.   As a mall but pretty rival specimen, less known, take he description of a fairy palace from Drayton's Nymphidia:—

> This palace standeth in the air,
> By necromancy placèd there,
> That it no tempests[4] needs to fear,
>   Which way soe'er it blow it:
> And somewhat southward tow'rd the noon,
> Whence lies a way up to the moon,
> And thence the Fairy can as soon
>   Pass to the earth below it.
> The walls of spiders' legs are made,
> Well mortisèd and finely laid;
> He was the master of his trade,
>   It curiously that builded:

---

[1] Meaning *The Quarrel of Oberon and Titania*, which Hunt extracts from the *Midsummer Night's Dream*, and prints in the volume to which this essay serves as introduction.

[2] I. 4. 59–62.

[3] In this and the following line Hunt prints 'Her.'   'The' s Pope's emendation.

[4] Hunt, 'tempest.'

The windows of the eyes of cats:

(because they see best at night,)

> And for the roof, instead of slats,
> Is covered with the skins of bats
> 5   *With moonshine that are gilded.*

Here also is a fairy bed, very delicate, from the same poet's Muse's Elysium:[1] —

> Of leaves of roses, *white and red,*
> Shall be the covering of her[2] bed;
> 10   The curtains, vallens, tester all
> Shall be the flower imperial;
> And for the fringe, it all along
> *With azure harebells shall be hung.*
> *Of lilies shall the pillows be.*
> 15   *With down stuft of the butterfly.*

Of fancy, so full of gusto as to border on imagination, Sir John Suckling, in his Ballad upon[3] a Wedding, has given some of the most playful and charming specimens in the language. 20 They glance like twinkles of the eye, or cherries bedewed: —

> *Her feet beneath her petticoat*
> *Like little mice stole in and out,*
> *As if they feared the light;*
> 25   But oh! she dances such a way!
> *No sun upon an Easter Day*
> Is half so fine a sight.

It is very daring, and has a sort of playful grandeur, to compare a lady's dancing with the 30 sun.   But as the sun has it all to himself in

---

[1] *Nymphal* 8, Cloris' first speech.
[2] Hunt, 'the.'   [3] Hunt, 'on.'

the heavens, so she, in the blaze of her beauty,
on earth. This is imagination fairly displac-
ing fancy. The following has enchanted everybody:—

> Her lips were red, *and one was thin*   5
> *Compared to* [1] *that was next her chin,*
> *Some bee had stung it newly.*

Every reader has stolen a kiss at that lip, gay or
grave.

With regard to the principle of Variety in 10
Uniformity by which verse ought to be modulated, and oneness of impression diversely produced, it has been contended by some that
Poetry need not be written in verse at all; that
prose is as good a medium, provided poetry be 15
conveyed through it; and that to think otherwise
is to confound letter with spirit, or form with
essence. But the opinion is a prosaical mistake.
Fitness and unfitness for *song*, or metrical excite-
ment, just make all the difference between a 20
poetical and prosaical subject; and the reason
why verse is necessary to the form of poetry is
that the perfection of poetical spirit demands it;
— that the circle of its enthusiasm, beauty, and
power, is incomplete without it. I do not mean 25
to say that a poet can never show himself a poet
in prose; but that, being one, his desire and
necessity will be to write in verse; and that, if
he were unable to do so, he would not, and could
not, deserve his title. Verse to the true poet is 30

---

[1] Hunt, ' with.'

41887

no clog.   It is idly called a trammel and a
difficulty.   It is a help.   It springs from the
same enthusiasm as the rest of his impulses, and
is necessary to their satisfaction and effect.
5 Verse is no more a clog than the condition of
·rushing upward is a clog to fire, or than the
roundness and order of the globe we live on is a
clog to the freedom and variety that abound
within its sphere.   Verse is no dominator over
10 the poet, except inasmuch as the bond is recip-
rocal, and the poet dominates over the verse.
They are lovers, playfully challenging each other's
rule, and delighted equally to rule and to obey.
Verse is the final proof to the poet that his
15 mastery over his art is complete.   It is the
shutting up of his powers in '*measureful* content';[1] the answer of form to his spirit; of
strength and ease to his guidance.   It is the
willing action, the proud and fiery happiness, of
20 the winged steed on whose back he has vaulted,

To[2] witch the world with noble[3] horsemanship.[4]

Verse, in short, is that finishing, and rounding,
and 'tuneful planeting' of the poet's creations,
which is produced of necessity by the smooth
25 tendencies of their energy or inward working,
and the harmonious dance into which they are
attracted round the orb of the beautiful.   Poetry,
in its complete sympathy with beauty, must of

[1] Adapted from *Macbeth* 2. 1. 17, 'measureless content.'
[2] Shakespeare has 'and.'
[3] Hunt, 'wondrous.'   [4] 1 *Henry IV.* 1. 1. 110.

necessity leave no sense of the beautiful, and no power over its forms, unmanifested; and verse flows as inevitably from this condition of its integrity, as other laws of proportion do from any other kind of embodiment of beauty (say that of 5 the human figure), however free and various the • movements may be that play within their limits. What great poet ever wrote his poems in prose? or where is a good prose poem, of any length, to be found?[1] The poetry of the Bible is under- 10 stood to be in verse, in the original.[2] Mr. Hazlitt has said a good word for those prose enlargements of some fine old song, which are known by the name of Ossian;[3] and in passages they deserve what he said; but he judiciously abstained from 15 saying anything about the form. Is Gesner's Death of Abel a poem? or Hervey's Meditations? The Pilgrim's Progress has been called one; and undoubtedly Bunyan had a genius which tended to make him a poet, and one of no mean order: 20 and yet it was of as ungenerous and low a sort as was compatible with so lofty an affinity; and this is the reason why it stopped where it did. He had a craving after the beautiful, but not enough of it in himself to echo to its music. On the 25 other hand, the possession of the beautiful will not be sufficient without force to utter it. The

[1] But cf. Sidney's *Defense of Poesy* 11 8-25; Shelley's *Defense* 7 33-10 7.

[2] Cf. my edition of *The Bible and English Prose Style*, pp. liv-lviii.

[3] Hazlitt, *Lectures on the English Poets*, close of chap. 1.

author of Telemachus [1] had a soul full of beauty
and tenderness.   He was not a man who, if he
had had a wife and children, would have run away
from them, as Bunyan's hero did, to get a place
5 by himself in heaven.   He was 'a little lower
than the angels,' [2] like our own Bishop Jewells [3]
and Berkeleys; [4] and yet he was no poet.   He
was too delicately, not to say feebly, absorbed in
his devotions to join in the energies of the
10 seraphic choir.

Every poet, then, is a versifier; every fine poet
an excellent one; and he is the best whose
verse exhibits the greatest amount of strength,
sweetness, straightforwardness, unsuperfluousness,
15 *variety*, and *oneness;* — oneness, that is to say,
consistency, in the general impression, metrical
and moral; and variety, or every pertinent
diversity of tone and rhythm, in the process.

Strength is the muscle of verse, and shows
20 itself in the number and force of the marked
syllables; as,

Sonorous metal blowing martial sounds. [5]

[1] Fénelon (1661–1715).

[2] Ps. 8. 5; Heb. 2. 7.

[3] See the testimonies to his worth in Russell's *Book of Authors*
(Chandos Classics), p. 21.

[4] Bishop Atterbury said of him: 'So much understanding, so
much knowledge, so much innocence, and so much humility I
did not think had been the portion of any but angels until I saw
this gentleman.'   Pope's lines are well known:

> 'Manners with candor are to Benson given,
> To Berkeley every virtue under heaven.'

[5] *P. L.* i. 540.   Hunt gives only 'Paradise Lost' in the text.

Behèmoth, biggest born of eàrth, ùphèaved
His vàstness.[1]

Blòw, winds, and cràck your chèeks! ràge! blòw!
You càtàràcts and hurricànoes, spòut
Till you have drènch'd our stèeples, dròwn'd the còcks! 5
You sùlphurous and thoùght-èxecuting fires,
Vaùnt-coùriers to òak-clèaving thùnderbòlts,
Singe my white hèad! And thòu, àll-shàking thùnder,
Smite [2] flàt the thick rotùndity o' the wòrld! [3]

Unexpected locations of the accent double this 10
force, and render it characteristic of passion and
abruptness. And here comes into play the
reader's corresponding fineness of ear, and his
retardations and accelerations in accordance with
those of the poet: — 15

> Then in the keyhole turns
> The intrïcăte wards, and every bolt and bar
> [Of massy iron or solid rock with ease] [4]
> Unfastens. On ă sŭddĕn òpen fly
> With impètuous recoil and jarring sound 20
> The infernal doors, and on their hinges grate
> Harsh thunder.[5]

> Abòmĭnăblĕ, inùttĕrăblĕ,[6] and worse
> Than fables yet have feigned.[7]

> Wàllŏwĭng ŭnwièldў, ĕnòrmous in their gait.[8] 25

Of unusual passionate accent, there is an
exquisite specimen in the Fairy Queen, where

[1] *P. L.* 7. 471–472. Hunt, 'Id.'
[2] Hunt, 'strike.'
[3] *King Lear* 3. 2. 1–7. Hunt has ' Lear.'
[4] Hunt omits without notice.
[5] *P. L.* 2. 876–882. Hunt has ' Par. Lost, Book II.'
[6] Hunt. ' unutterable.'
[7] *P. L.* 2. 626–627. Hunt, 'Id.'   [8] *P. L.* 7. 411.

Una is lamenting her desertion by the Red-Cross Knight : —

> But he, my Lyon, and my noble Lord,
> How does he find in cruell hart to hate
> 5   Her, that him lov'd, and ever most adord
> *As the Gòd of my lîfe?*   Why hath he me abhord?[1]

See the whole stanza, with a note upon it, in the present volume.[2]

The abuse of strength is harshness and heavi-
10 ness; the reverse of it is weakness.   There is a noble sentiment — it appears both in Daniel's and Sir John Beaumont's works, but is most probably the latter's — which is a perfect outrage of strength in the sound of the words: —

> 15   Only the firmest and the *constant'st* hearts
> God sets to act the *stout'st* and hardest parts.[8]

Stout'st and *constant'st* for 'stoutest' and 'most constant!'   It is as bad as the intentional crabbedness of the line in Hudibras:[4] —

> 20   He that hangs or *beats out's* brains,
> The devil's in him if *he* feigns.

Beats out's brains, for 'beats out his brains.'   Of heaviness, Davenant's Gondibert is a formidable specimen, almost throughout: —

> 25 With silence (òrder's help, and màrk of càre)
>   They chìd[5] thàt nòise which hèedless yòuth effèct;[6]
>   Stìll coùrse for ùse, for hèalth thèy clèanlyness[7] wère,
>   And sàve in wèllfìxed àrms, all nìceness chècked.

---

[1] *F. Q.* 1. 3. 7.   [2] Cf. p. 35, note 1.
[8] This quotation I have not succeeded it finding.
[4] 2. 10. 497–498.   [5] Hunt, 'chide.'   [6] Hunt, 'affect.'
[7] Hunt, 'cleanness.'

Thèy thoùght, thòse that, unàrmed, expòsed fràil lìfe,
But nàked nàture vàliantly betràyed;
Whò wàs, though nàked, sàfe, till prìde màde strìfe,
But màde defènse must ùse, nòw dànger's màde.[1]

And so he goes digging and lumbering on, like a 5
heavy preacher thumping the pulpit in italics, and
spoiling many ingenious reflections.

Weakness in versification is want of accent and
<u>emphasis.</u> It generally accompanies prosaical-
ness, and is the consequence of weak thoughts, 10
and of the affectation of a certain well-bred
enthusiasm. The writings of the late Mr. Hayley
were remarkable for it; and it abounds among the
lyrical imitators of Cowley, and the whole of what
is called our French school of poetry, when it 15
aspired above its wit and ' sense.' It sometimes
breaks down in a horrible, hopeless manner, as
if giving way at the first step. The following
ludicrous passage in Congreve, intended to be
particularly fine, contains an instance: — 20

And lo! Silence himself is here:
Methinks I see the midnight god appear.
In all his downy pomp arrayed,
Behold the reverend shade.
An ancient sigh he sits upon!!! 25
Whose memory of sound is long since gone.
And purposely annihilated for his throne!!![2]

See also the would-be enthusiasm of Addison
about music: —

---

[1] Canto 3. sts. 8, 9.
[2] 'Ode on the singing of Mrs. Arabella Hunt.' Hunt inserts
in text.

> For ever consecrate the *day*
> To music and *Cecilia ;*
> Music, the greatest good that mortals know,
> And all of heaven we have below,
> Music can noble HINTS *impart ! ! !* [1]

It is observable that the unpoetic masters of
ridicule are apt to make the most ridiculous
mistakes, when they come to affect a strain
higher than the one they are accustomed to.
But no wonder.   Their habits neutralize the
enthusiasm it requires.

Sweetness, though not identical with smoothness, any more than feeling is with sound, always
includes it; and smoothness is a thing so little to
be regarded for its own sake, and indeed so worth-
less in poetry, but for some taste of sweetness,
that I have not thought necessary to mention it
by itself; though such an all-in-all in versification
was it regarded not a hundred years back, that
Thomas Warton, himself an idolater of Spenser,
ventured to wish the following line in the Fairy
Queen,

Yet [2] was admirèd much of fooles, *wòmen,* and boys [3] —

altered to

25   Yet was admirèd much of women, fools, and boys —

thus destroying the fine scornful emphasis on the
first syllable of ' women!' (an ungallant intima-

---

[1] *A Song for St. Cecilia's Day at Oxford,* **str.** 3.
[2] Hunt, ' And.'
[3] *F. Q.* 5. 2. 30.

tion, by the way, against the fair sex, very
startling in this no less woman-loving than great
poet). Any poetaster can be smooth. Smoothness abounds in all small poets, as sweetness does
in the greater. Sweetness is the smoothness of
grace and delicacy — of the sympathy with the
pleasing and lovely. Spenser is full of it —
Shakespeare — Beaumont and Fletcher — Coleridge. Of Spenser's and Coleridge's versification it is the prevailing characteristic. Its main
secrets are a smooth progression between variety
and sameness, and a voluptuous sense of the
continuous — 'linked sweetness long drawn out.' [1]
Observe the first and last lines of the stanza in
the Fairy Queen, describing a shepherd brushing
away the gnats; — the open and the close *e*'s in
the one,

As gèntle shèpheard in swēēte ēventide [2] —

and the repetition of the word *oft*, and the fall
from the vowel *a* into the two *u*'s in the other, —

He [3] brusheth *oft*, and *oft* doth màr their mùrmùrings.

So in his description of two substances in the
handling, both equally smooth, —

Each smoother seems than each, and each than each seems
smoother. [4]

An abundance of examples from his poetry will
be found in the volume before us. His beauty
revolves on itself with conscious loveliness. And

[1] *L'Allegro* i 39.
[2] *F. Q.* 1. 1. 23.
[3] Hunt, 'She.'
[4] I have not found this.

Coleridge is worthy to be named with him, as the reader will see also, and has seen already. Let him take a sample meanwhile from the poem called the Day-Dream! Observe both the variety
5 and sameness of the vowels, and the repetition of the soft consonants:—

> My eyes make pictures when they are [1] shut:—
>   I see a fountain, large and fair,
>   A willow and a ruined hut.
> 10   And *thee* and *me* and Mary there.
> *O Mary! make thy gentle lap our pillow;*
> *Bend o'er us, like a bower, my beautiful green willow.*

By *Straightforwardness* is meant the flow of words in their natural order, free alike from mere
15 prose, and from those inversions to which bad poets recur in order to escape the charge of prose, but chiefly to accommodate their rimes. In Shadwell's play of Psyche,[2] Venus gives the sisters of the heroine an answer, of which the
20 following is the *entire* substance, literally, in so many words. The author had nothing better for her to say:—

> I receive your prayers with kindness, and will give suc-
> cess to your hopes. I have seen, with anger, mankind adore
> 25 your sister's beauty and deplore her scorn: which they shall
> do no more. For I'll so resent their idolatry, as shall con-
> tent your wishes to the full.

Now in default of all imagination, fancy, and expression, how was the writer to turn these
30 words into poetry or rime? Simply by diverting

---

[1] Hunt, 'they 're.'   [2] Published in 1674.

them from their natural order, and twisting the
halves of the sentences each before the other.

> With kindness I your prayers receive,
> And to your hopes success will give.
> I have, with anger, seen mankind adore   5
> Your sister's beauty and her scorn deplore;
>   Which they shall do no more.
> For their idolatry I'll so resent,
> As shall your wishes to the full content!!¹

This is just as if a man were to allow that there 10
was no poetry in the words, 'How do you find
yourself?' 'Very well, I thank you;' but to hold
them inspired, if altered into

> Yourself how do you find?
> Very well, you I thank.²   15

It is true, the best writers in Shadwell's age
were addicted to these inversions, partly for their
own reasons, as far as rime was concerned, and
partly because they held it to be writing in the
classical and Virgilian manner. What has since 20
been called Artificial Poetry was then flourishing,
in contradistinction to Natural; or Poetry seen
chiefly through art and books, and not in its first
sources. But when the artificial poet partook of

---

¹ Venus' Song in Act 1.

² In his Preface, Hunt alludes to the unintentional similarity
of this comparison with a note of Coleridge's in the *Biographia
Literaria* (p. 186 of the Bohn edition): 'As the ingenious gentleman under the influence of the Tragic Muse contrived to dislo-
cate, "I wish you a good morning, sir!" "Thank you, sir, and
I wish you the same," into two blank-verse heroics:

> To you a morning good, good sir! I wish.
> You, sir! I thank; to you the same wish I.'

the natural, or, in other words, was a true poet
after his kind, his best was always written in his
most natural and straightforward manner.   Hear
Shadwell's antagonist Dryden.   Not a particle of
5 inversion, beyond what is used for the sake of
emphasis in common discourse, and this only in
one line (the last but three), is to be found in his
immortal character of the Duke of Buckingham: —

> A man so various, that he seemed to be
> 10 Not one, but all mankind's epitome:
> Stiff in opinions, *always in the wrong,*
> *Was everything by starts, and nothing long;*
> But in the course of one revolving moon
> Was chemist, fiddler, statesman, and buffoon;
> 15 Then all for women, painting, riming,[1] drinking,
> *Besides ten thousand freaks that died in thinking.*
> *Blest madman!* who could every hour employ
> *With something new to wish or to enjoy!*
> Railing and praising were his usual themes,
> 20 And both, to show his judgment, in extremes:
> So over-violent or over-civil
> *That every man with him was God or Devil.*
> In squandering wealth was his peculiar art;
> *Nothing went unrewarded, but desert.*
> 25 Beggared by fools whom still he found too late,
> *He had his jest, and they had his estate.*[2]

Inversion itself was often turned into a grace
in these poets, and may be in others, by the
power of being superior to it; using it only with
30 a classical air, and as a help lying next to them,
instead of a salvation which they are obliged to

---

[1] Hunt, 'riming, dancing.'
[2] *Absalom and Achitophel* 545–562.

seek. In jesting passages also it sometimes gave
the rime a turn agreeably wilful, or an appearance of choosing what lay in its way; as if a man
should pick up a stone to throw at another's head,
where a less confident foot would have stumbled 5
over it.   Such is Dryden's use of the word *might*
—the mere sign of a tense—in his pretended
ridicule of the monkish practice of rising to sing
psalms in the night.

> And much they grieved to see so nigh their hall 10
> The bird that warned St. Peter of his fall;
> That he should raise his mitred crest on high,
> And clap his wings and call his family
> To sacred rites: and vex the ethereal powers
> With midnight matins at uncivil hours; 15
> Nay more, his quiet neighbors should molest
> *Just in the sweetness of their morning rest.*

(What a line full of 'another doze' is that!)

> *Beast of a bird!* supinely when he *might*
> Lie snug and sleep, to rise before the light! 20
> What if his dull forefathers used that cry?
> Could he not let a bad example die?[1]

I the more gladly quote instances like those of
Dryden to illustrate the points in question,
because they are specimens of the very highest 25
kind of writing in the heroic couplet upon subjects
not heroical.   As to prosaicalness in general, it is
sometimes indulged in by young writers on the
plea of its being natural; but this is a mere
confusion of triviality with propriety, and is 30
usually the result of indolence.

[1] *The Hind and the Panther* 3. 1005-1016.

Unsuperfluousness is rather a matter of style in
general, than of the sound and order of words:
and yet versification is so much strengthened by
it, and so much weakened by its opposite, that it
5 could not but come within the category of its
requisites. When superfluousness of words is not
occasioned by overflowing animal spirits, as in
Beaumont and Fletcher, or by the very genius of
luxury, as in Spenser (in which cases it is enrich-
10 ment as well as overflow), there is no worse sign
for a poet altogether, except pure barrenness.
Every word that could be taken away from a
poem, unreferable to either of the above reasons
for it, is a damage; and many such are death;
15 for there is nothing that posterity seems so
determined to resent as this want of respect for
its time and trouble. The world is too rich in
books to endure it. Even true poets have died of
this Writer's Evil. Trifling ones have survived,
20 with scarcely any pretensions but the terseness of
their trifles. What hope can remain for wordy
mediocrity? Let the discerning reader take up
any poem, pen in hand, for the purpose of
discovering how many words he can strike out
25 of it that give him no requisite ideas, no relevant
ones that he cares for, and no reasons for the
rime beyond its necessity, and he will see what
blot and havoc he will make in many an admired
production of its day — what marks of its inevita-
30 ble fate. Bulky authors in particular, however
safe they may think themselves, would do well to

consider what parts of their cargo they might dispense with in their proposed voyage down the gulfs of time; for many a gallant vessel, though indestructible in its age, has perished; — many a load of words, expected to be in eternal demand, 5 gone to join the wrecks of self-love, or rotted in the warehouses of change and vicissitude. I have said the more on this point, because in an age when the true inspiration has undoubtedly been re-awakened by Coleridge and his fellows, and we 10 have so many new poets coming forward, it may be as well to give a general warning against that tendency to an accumulation and ostentation of *thoughts*,[1] which is meant to be a refutation in full of the pretensions of all poetry less cogitabund, 15 whatever may be the requirements of its class. Young writers should bear in mind, that even some of the very best materials for poetry are not poetry built; and that the smallest marble shrine, of exquisite workmanship, outvalues all 20 that architect ever chipped away. Whatever can be so dispensed with is rubbish.

Variety in versification consists in whatsoever can be done for the prevention of monotony, by diversity of stops and cadences, distribution of 25 emphasis, and retardation and acceleration of time; for the whole real secret of versification is a musical secret, and is not attainable to any vital effect save by the ear of genius. All the mere knowledge of feet and numbers, of accent 30

---

[1] Cf. some of Browning's poetry, for instance.

and quantity, will no more impart it, than a
knowledge of the Guide to Music will make a
Beethoven or a Paisiello.   It is a matter of
sensibility and imagination; of the beautiful in
5 poetical passion, accompanied by musical; of the
imperative necessity for a pause here, and a
cadence there, and a quicker or slower utterance
in this or that place, created by analogies of
sound with sense, by the fluctuations of feeling,
10 by the demands of the gods and graces that visit
the poet's harp, as the winds visit that of Æolus.
The same time and quantity which are occasioned
by the spiritual part of this secret, thus become
its formal ones — not feet and syllables, long and
15 short, iambics or trochees; which are the reduc-
tion of it to its *less* than dry bones.   You might
get, for instance, not only ten and eleven, but
thirteen or fourteen syllables into a riming, as
well as blank, heroical verse, if time and the
20 feeling permitted; and in irregular measure this
is often done; just as musicians put twenty notes
in a bar instead of two, quavers instead of minims,
according as the feeling they are expressing
impels them to fill up the time with short and
25 hurried notes, or with long; or as the choristers
in a cathedral retard or precipitate the words of
the chant, according as the quantity of its notes,
and the colon which divides the verse of the
psalm, conspire to demand it.   Had the moderns
30 borne this principle in mind when they settled
the prevailing systems of verse, instead of learning

them, as they appear to have done, from the first drawling and one-syllabled notation of the church hymns, we should have retained all the advantages of the more numerous versification of the ancients, without being compelled to fancy that there was 5 no alternative for us between our syllabical uniformity and the hexameters or other special forms unsuited to our tongues. But to leave this question alone, we will present the reader with a few sufficing specimens of the difference between 10 monotony and variety in versification, first from Pope, Dryden, and Milton, and next from Gay and Coleridge. The following is the boasted melody of the nevertheless exquisite poet of the Rape of the Lock — exquisite in his wit and fancy, though 15 not in his numbers. The reader will observe that it is literally *see-saw*, like the rising and falling of a plank, with a light person at one end who is jerked up in the briefer time, and a heavier one who is set down more leisurely at the other. 20 It is in the otherwise charming description of the heroine of that poem : —

> On her white breast — a sparkling cross she wore,
> Which Jews might kiss — and infidels adore;
> Her lively looks — a sprightly mind disclose,   25
> Quick as her eyes — and as unfixed as those.
> Favors to none — to all she smiles extends,
> Oft she rejects — but never once offends;
> Bright as the sun — her eyes the gazers strike,
> And like the sun — they shine on all alike: 30
> Yet graceful ease — and sweetness void of pride,
> Might hide her faults — if belles had faults to hide;

If to her share — some female errors fall,
Look on her face — and you'll forget 'em all.[1]

Compare with this the description of Iphigenia
in one of Dryden's stories from Boccaccio: —

5 It happened — on a summer's holiday,
That to the greenwood shade — he took his way,
For Cymon shunned the church — and used not much
    to pray:
His quarter-staff — which he could ne'er forsake,
10 Hung half before — and half behind his back.
He trudged along — unknowing[2] what he sought,
And whistled as he went — for want of thought.

By chance conducted — or by thirst constrained,
The deep recesses of the[3] grove he gained; —
15 Where — in a plain defended by the[3] wood.
Crept through the matted grass — a crystal flood,
By which — an alabaster fountain stood;
And on the margent of the fount was laid —
Attended by her slaves — a sleeping maid;
20 Like Dian and her nymphs — when, tired with sport,
To rest by cool Eurotas they resort. —
The dame herself — the goddess well expressed,
Not more distinguished by her purple vest —
Than by the charming features of her[4] face —
25 And, even[5] in slumber — a superior grace:
Her comely limbs — composed with decent care,
Her body shaded — with a slight[6] cymarr,
Her bosom to the view - - was only bare;
Where two beginning paps were scarcely spied, —
30 For yet their places were but signified. —

[1] *Rape of the Lock* 2. 7–18.   [4] Hunt, 'the.'
[2] Hunt, 'not knowing.'   [5] Hunt, 'e'en.'
[3] Hunt, 'a.'   [6] Hunt, 'by a light.'

The fanning wind upon her bosom blows, —
To meet the fanning wind —the bosom rose;
The fanning wind — and purling streams [1] — continue
    her repose.[2]

For a further variety take, from the same
author's Theodore and Honoria, a passage in
which the couplets are run one into the other,
and all of it modulated, like the former, according
to the feeling demanded by the occasion: —

Whilst listening to the murmuring leaves he stood —   10
More than a mile immersed within the wood —
At once the wind was laid. | — The whispering sound
Was dumb. | — A rising earthquake rocked the ground.
With deeper brown the grove was overspread —
A sudden horror seized his giddy head —   15
And his ears tinkled — and his color fled.

Nature was in alarm. — Some danger nigh
Seemed threatened —though unseen to mortal eye.
Unused to fear — he summoned all his soul,
And stood collected in himself — and whole :   20
Not long.[3] —

But for a crowning specimen of variety of pause
and accent, apart from emotion, nothing can
surpass the account, in Paradise Lost, of the
Devil's search for an accomplice: —   25

           There was a plàce,
(Nòw nòt — though Sìn — not Tìme — first wroùght
    the chànge)
Where Tìgris — at the foot of Pàradise,
Into a gùlf — shòt under ground — till pàrt   30
Ròse up a foùntain by the Trèe of Life.
In with the river sunk — and *with it ròse*
Sàtan — invòlved in rìsing mìst — then soùght

[1] Hunt, 'stream.'   [2] *Cymon and Iphigenia* 79-106.
[3] *Theodore and Honoria* 88-99.

Whère to lie hìd. — Sèa he had searched —- and lànd
From Eden over Pòntus — and the Pòol
Mæòtis — *ùp* beyond the river *Ob;*
Dòwnward as fàr antàrctic: — and in lèngth
5 West from Oròntes — to the òcean bàrred
At Dàriën — thènce to the lànd whère flòws
Gànges and Indus. — Thùs the òrb he ròamed
With nàrrow sèarch, — and with inspèction deep
Considered èvery crèature — whìch of àll
10 Mòst opportùne mìght sèrve his wìles — and foùnd
The Sèrpent — sùbtlest bèast of all the fìeld.[1]

If the reader cast his eye again over this passage,
he will not find a verse in it which is not varied
and harmonized in the most remarkable manner.
15 Let him notice in particular that curious balancing
of the lines in the sixth and tenth verses: —

> *In* with the river sunk, &c.

and

> *Up* beyond the river *Ob.*

20   It might, indeed, be objected to the versification of Milton, that it exhibits too constant a
perfection of this kind.   It sometimes forces
upon us too great a sense of consciousness on
the part of the composer.   We miss the first
25 sprightly runnings of verse — the ease and
sweetness of spontaneity.   Milton, I think, also
too often condenses weight into heaviness.

Thus much concerning the chief of our two
most popular measures.   The other, called octo-
30 syllabic, or the measure of eight syllables, offered
such facilities for *namby-pamby*, that it had become
a jest as early as the time of Shakespeare, who

[1] *P. L.* 9. 69–86.

makes Touchstone call it the 'butter-woman's rank [1] to market,' and the 'very false gallop of verses.' [2] It has been advocated, in opposition to the heroic measure, upon the ground that ten syllables lead a man into epithets and other superfluities, [5] while eight syllables compress him into a sensible and pithy gentleman. But the heroic measure laughs at it. So far from compressing, it converts one line into two, and sacrifices everything to the quick and importunate return of the rime. [10] With Dryden compare Gay, even in the strength of Gay : [3] —

> The wind was high, the window shakes:
> With sudden start the miser wakes;
> Along the silent room he stalks, [15]

(A miser never 'stalks;' but a rime was desired for 'walks')

> Looks back, and trembles as he walks:
> Each lock and every bolt he tries.
> In every creek and corner pries: [20]
> Then opes the chest with treasure stored,
> And stands in rapture o'er his hoard;

('Hoard' and 'treasure stored' are just made for one another,)

> But now, with sudden qualms possessed, [25]
> He wrings his hands, he beats his breast;
> By conscience stung, he wildly stares,
> And thus his guilty soul declares.

[1] Hunt, 'rate.'

[2] *As You Like It* 3. 2. 103, 119. Hunt confuses the seven-syllabled trochaic (and that on a single riming sound) with the eight-syllabled iambic.

[3] *Fable Sixth.*

And so he denounces his gold, as miser never denounced it; and sighs because

Virtue resides on earth no more!

Coleridge saw the mistake which had been made with regard to this measure, and restored it to the beautiful freedom of which it was capable, by calling to mind the liberties allowed its old musical professors the minstrels, and dividing it by *time* instead of *syllables;* — by the *beat of four*, into which you might get as many syllables as you could, instead of allotting eight syllables to the poor time, whatever it might have to say.   He varied it further with alternate rimes and stanzas, with rests and omissions precisely analogous to those in music, and rendered it altogether worthy to utter the manifold thoughts and feelings of himself and his lady Christabel.   He even ventures, with an exquisite sense of solemn strangeness and license (for there is witchcraft going forward), to introduce a couplet of blank verse, itself as mystically and beautifully modulated as anything in the music of Glück or Weber: —

> 'Tis the middle of night by the castle clock,
> And the owls have awakened the crowing cock;
> Tu — whit! — Tu — whoo!
> And hark. again! the crowing cock,
> *How drowsily it*[1] *crew.*
> Sir Leoline. the baron rich,
> Hath a toothless mastiff, which[2]

---

[1] Hunt, 'he.'   [2] Hunt, 'bitch.'

From her kennel beneath the rock
Maketh [1] answer to the clock,
Four for the quarters, and twelve for the hour,
Ever and aye, by shine and shower,
Sixteen short howls, not over loud;   5
Some say, she sees my lady's shroud.

Is the night chilly and dark?
The night is chilly, but not dark.
The thin gray cloud is spread on high,
It covers but not hides the sky.   10
The moon is behind, and at the full,
And yet she looks both small and dull.
The night is chill,[2] the cloud is gray;

(These are not superfluities, but mysterious
returns of importunate feeling)   15

'Tis a month before the month of May,
And the Spring comes slowly up this way.
The lovely lady, Christabel,
Whom her father loves so well,
What makes her in the wood so late,   20
A furlong from the castle-gate?
She had dreams all yesternight
Of her own betrothèd knight;
And she in the midnight wood will pray
For the weal of her lover that's far away.   25

She stole along, she nothing spoke,
The sighs she heaved were soft and low,
And naught was green upon the oak,
But moss and rarest misletoe;
She kneels beneath the huge oak tree,   30
And in silence prayeth she.

---

[1] Hunt, 'She maketh.'   [2] Hunt, 'chilly.'

The lady sprang up suddenly,
The lovely lady, Christabel!
It moaned as near as near can be,
But what it is, she cannot tell. —
5   On the other side it seems to be
Of thĕ hùge, broàd-breàsted, òld oàk trèe.

The night is chill; the forest bare;
Is it the wind that moaneth bleak?

(This 'bleak moaning' is a witch's)

10   There is not wind enough in the air
To move away the ringlet curl
From the lovely lady's cheek —
There is not wind enough to twirl
The òne rĕd lĕaf, the làst ŏf ĭts clàn
15   *That dàncĕs ăs ŏftĕn ăs dànce it càn,*
Hàngĭng sŏ light and hàngĭng sŏ hìgh,
On thĕ tòpmost twìg thăt lŏoks ùp ăt thĕ skỳ.

Hush, beating heart of Christabel!
Jesu Maria, shield her well!
20   She folded her arms beneath her cloak,
And stole to the other side of the oak.
        What sees she there?

There she sees a damsel bright,
Drest in a silken robe of white.[1]
25   That shadowy in the moonlight shone:
The neck that made that white robe wan,
Her stately neck and arms were bare;
Her blue-veined feet unsandaled were;
And wildly glittered here and there
30   The gems entangled in her hair.
I guess 'twas *frightful* there to see
A lady so richly clad as she —
Beautiful exceedingly.

[1] Hunt, 'Dressed in a robe of silken white.'

The principle of Variety in Uniformity is here worked out in a style 'beyond the reach of art.'[1] Everything is diversified according to the demand of the moment, of the sounds, the sights, the emotions; the very uniformity of the outline is 5 gently varied; and yet we feel that *the whole is one and of the same character,* the single and sweet unconsciousness of the heroine making all the rest seem more conscious, and ghastly, and expectant. It is thus that *versification itself* 10 *becomes part of the sentiment of a poem,* and vindicates the pains that have been taken to show its importance. I know of no very fine versification unaccompanied with fine poetry; no poetry of a mean order accompanied with verse of the 15 highest.

As to Rime, which might be thought too insignificant to mention, it is not at all so. The universal consent of modern Europe, and of the East in all ages, has made it one of the musical 20 beauties of verse for all poetry but epic and dramatic, and even for the former with Southern Europe — a sustainment for the enthusiasm, and a demand to enjoy. The mastery of it consists in never writing it for its own sake, or at least never 25 appearing to do so; in knowing how to vary it, to give it novelty, to render it more or less strong, to divide it (when not in couplets) at the proper intervals, to repeat it many times where luxury or animal spirits demand it (see an instance in 30

[1] Pope, *Essay on Criticism* 153.

Titania's speech to the Fairies[1]), to impress an
affecting or startling remark with it, and to make
it, in comic poetry, a new and surprising addition
to the jest.

5   Large was his bounty and his soul sincere,
           Heaven did a recompense as largely send;
       He gave to misery all he had, *a tear;*
           He gained from heaven ('twas all he wished) *a friend.*[2]

       The fops are proud of scandal; for they cry
10   At every lewd, low character, — 'That's *I.*'[3]

       What makes all doctrines plain and clear?
       About two hundred pounds a year.
       And that which was proved true before,
       Prove false again? *Two hundred more.*[4]

15   Compound for sins they are *inclined to,*
       By damning those they have *no mind to.*[5]

           – Stored with deletery *med'cines,*
       Which whosoever took is *dead since.*[6]

Sometimes it is a grace in a master like Butler to
20 force his rime, thus showing a laughing wilful
power over the most stubborn materials: —

                                        Win
           The women, and make them draw in
           The men, as Indians with a *female*
25   Tame elephant inveigle *the* male.[7]

---

[1] *Midsummer Night's Dream* 3. 1. 172 ff.

[2] *Gray's Elegy.* Hunt inserts the *general* reference in the text,
as in all these instances.

[3] Dryden, Prologue to the *Pilgrim* of Fletcher. (Scott's ed.
of Dryden, 8 411.)

[4] *Hudibras* 3. 1. 1277–1280.   [6] *Hud.* 1. 4. 317–318.

[5] *Hud.* 1. 1. 215–216.   [7] *Hud.* 1. 2. 587–588.

> He made an instrument to know
> If the moon shines at full or no;
> That would, as soon as e'er she *shone, straight*
> Whether 'twere day or night *demonstrate;*
> Tell what her diameter to an *inch is,*   5
> And prove that she's not made of *green cheese.*[1]

Pronounce it, by all means, *grinches*, to make the joke more wilful. The happiest triple rime, perhaps, that ever was written, is in Don Juan:—

> But oh! ye lords of ladies *intellectual*,   10
> Inform us truly, — haven't they *hen-pecked you all?*[2]

The sweepingness of the assumption completes the flowing breadth of effect.

Dryden confessed that a rime often gave him a thought.[3] Probably the happy word 'sprung' in 15 the following passage from Ben Jonson was suggested by it; but then the poet must have had the feeling in him:—

> — Let our trumpets sound,
> And cleave both air and ground
>   With beating of our drums.   20
> Let every lyre be strung,
> Harp, lute, theorbo, *sprung*
>   *With touch of dainty thumbs.*[4]

Boileau's trick for appearing to rime naturally 25 was to compose the second line of his couplet first! which gives one the crowning idea of the

---

[1] *Hud.* 2. 3. 261–266.

[2] *Don Juan*, Canto 1. st. 22.

[3] Perhaps referring to his *Essay of Dramatic Poesy*, near the beginning of Neander's defense of rime.

[4] *An Ode, or Song, by all the Muses, in celebration of her Majesty's Birthday, 1630.* For 'dainty' Gifford reads 'learned.'

'artificial school of poetry.'   Perhaps the most
perfect master of rime, the easiest and most
abundant, was the greatest writer of comedy
that the world has seen — Molière.[1]

5   If a young reader should ask, after all, What is
the quickest way of knowing bad poets from good,
the best poets from the next best, and so on? the
answer is, the only and twofold way: first, the
perusal of the best poets with the greatest atten-
10 tion; and, second, the cultivation of that love of
truth and beauty which made them what they are.
Every true reader of poetry partakes a more than
ordinary portion of the poetic nature; and no one
can be completely such, who does not love, or
15 take an interest in, everything that interests the
poet, from the firmament to the daisy — from the
highest heart of man to the most pitiable of the
low.   It is a good practice to read with pen in
hand, marking what is liked or doubted.   It
20 rivets the attention, realizes the greatest amount
of enjoyment, and facilitates reference.   It
enables the reader also, from time to time, to
see what progress he makes with his own mind,
and how it grows up towards the stature of its
25 exalter.

If the same person should ask, What class of
poetry is the highest?   I should say, undoubtedly,
the epic;[2] for it includes the drama, with narration besides; or the speaking and action of the

---

[1] *Cf.* Boileau, *Satire* 2.

[2] See Sidney's *Defense* 30 27, and note; on the other side
Aristotle's *Poetics*, near the end.

characters, with the speaking of the poet himself,
whose utmost address is taxed to relate all well
for so long a time, particularly in the passages
least sustained by enthusiasm. Whether this
class has included the greatest poet, is another 5
question still under trial; for Shakespeare per-
plexes all such verdicts, even when the claimant
is Homer; though, if a judgment may be drawn
from his early narratives (Venus and Adonis, and
the Rape of Lucrece), it is to be doubted whether 10
even Shakespeare could have told a story like
Homer, owing to that incessant activity and
superfœtation of thought, a little less of which
might be occasionally desired even in his plays;
—if it were possible, once possessing anything 15
of his, to wish it away. Next to Homer and
Shakespeare come such narrators as the less
universal, but still intenser Dante; Milton, with
his dignified imagination; the universal, pro-
foundly simple Chaucer; and luxuriant, remote 20
Spenser — immortal child in poetry's most poetic
solitudes: then the great second-rate dramatists;
unless those who are better acquainted with Greek
tragedy than I am, demand a place for them before
Chaucer: then the airy, yet robust universality of 25
Ariosto; the hearty, out-of-door nature of Theo-
critus, also a universalist; the finest lyrical poets
(who only take short flights, compared with the
narrators); the purely contemplative poets who
have more thought than feeling; the descriptive, 30
satirical, didactic, epigrammatic.[1] It is to be borne

---

[1] *Cf.* Sidney, *Defense* 9 34 ff.

in mind, however, that the first poet of an inferior
class may be superior to followers in the train of
a higher one, though the superiority is by no
means to be taken for granted; otherwise Pope
5 would be superior to Fletcher, and Butler to Pope.
Imagination, teeming with action and character,
makes the greatest poets; feeling and thought the
next; fancy (by itself) the next; wit the last.
Thought by itself makes no poet at all; for the
10 mere conclusions of the understanding can at
best be only so many intellectual matters of fact.
Feeling, even destitute of conscious thought,
stands a far better poetical chance; feeling being
a sort of thought without the process of thinking
15 —a grasper of the truth without seeing it. And
what is very remarkable, feeling seldom makes
the blunders that thought does. An idle distinction has been made between taste and judgment.
Taste is the very maker of judgment. Put an
20 artificial fruit in your mouth, or only handle it,
and you will soon perceive the difference between
judging from taste or tact, and judging from the
abstract figment called judgment. The latter
does but throw you into guesses and doubts.
25 Hence the conceits that astonish us in the
gravest, and even subtlest thinkers, whose taste
is not proportionate to their mental perceptions:
men like Donne, for instance; who, apart from
accidental personal impressions, seem to look at
30 nothing as it really is, but only as to what may
be thought of it. Hence, on the other hand, the

delightfulness of those poets who never violate truth of feeling, whether in things real or imaginary; who are always consistent with their object and its requirements; and who run the great round of nature, not to perplex and be perplexed, but to make themselves and us happy. And luckily, delightfulness is not incompatible with greatness, willing soever as men may be in their present imperfect state to set the power to subjugate above the power to please. Truth, of any great kind whatsoever, makes great writing. This is the reason why such poets as Ariosto, though not writing with a constant detail of thought and feeling like Dante, are justly considered great as well as delightful. Their greatness proves itself by the same truth of nature, and sustained power, though in a different way. Their action is not so crowded and weighty; their sphere has more territories less fertile; but it has enchantments of its own, which excess of thought would spoil — luxuries, laughing graces, animal spirits; and not to recognize the beauty and greatness of these, treated as they treat them, is simply to be defective in sympathy. Every planet is not Mars or Saturn. There is also Venus and Mercury. There is one genius of the south, and another of the north, and others uniting both. The reader who is too thoughtless or too sensitive to like intensity of any sort, and he who is too thoughtful or too dull to like anything but the greatest possible stimulus of reflection or passion,

are equally wanting in complexional fitness for a
thorough enjoyment of books. Ariosto occasionally says as fine things as Dante, and Spenser as
Shakespeare; but the business of both is to enjoy;
5 and in order to partake their enjoyment to its full
extent, you must feel what poetry is in the general
as well as the particular, must be aware that there
are different songs of the spheres, some fuller of
notes, and others of a sustained delight; and as
10 the former keep you perpetually alive to thought
or passion, so from the latter you receive a constant harmonious sense of truth and beauty, more
agreeable perhaps on the whole, though less
exciting. Ariosto, for instance, does not *tell
15 a story* with the brevity and concentrated passion
of Dante; every sentence is not so full of matter,
nor the style so removed from the indifference
of prose; yet you are charmed with a truth of
another sort, equally characteristic of the writer,
20 equally drawn from nature and substituting a
healthy sense of enjoyment for intenser emotion.
Exclusiveness of liking for this or that mode of
truth, only shows, either that a reader's perceptions are limited, or that he would sacrifice truth
25 itself to his favorite form of it. Sir Walter
Raleigh, who was as trenchant with his pen as
his sword, hailed the Faery Queen of his friend
Spenser in verses in which he said that Petrarch
was thenceforward to be no more heard of;[1] and

[1] All suddenly I saw the Faery Queene;
   At whose approch the soule of Petrarke wept,
   And from thenceforth those graces were not seene.

that in all English poetry there was nothing he
counted 'of any price' but the effusions of the
new author.[1] Yet Petrarch is still living; Chaucer
was not abolished by Sir Walter; and Shakespeare
is thought somewhat valuable. A botanist might 5
as well have said that myrtles and oaks were to
disappear, because acacias had come up. It is
with the poet's creations as with Nature's, great
or small. Wherever truth and beauty, whatever
their amount, can be worthily shaped into verse, 10
and answer to some demand for it in our hearts,
there poetry is to be found; whether in productions grand and beautiful as some great event, or
some mighty, leafy solitude, or no bigger and more
pretending than a sweet face or a bunch of violets; 15
whether in Homer's epic or Gray's Elegy, in the
enchanted gardens of Ariosto and Spenser, or the
very pot-herbs[2] of the Schoolmistress of Shen-
stone, the balms of the simplicity of a cottage.
Not to know and feel this is to be deficient in the 20
universality of Nature herself, who is a poetess on
the smallest as well as the largest scale, and who
calls upon us to admire all her productions; not
indeed with the same degree of admiration, but
with no refusal of it, except to defect. 25

I cannot draw this essay towards its conclusion better than with three memorable words of
Milton; who has said, that poetry, in comparison

---

[1] Of me no lines are loved, nor letters are of price,
   Of all which speak our English tongue, but those of thy
      device.
[2] *The Schoolmistress* sts. 11, 12, 13.

with science,[1] is 'simple, sensuous, and passionate.'
By simple, he means unperplexed and self-evident;
by sensuous, genial and full of imagery; by pas-.
sionate, excited and enthusiastic. I am aware
that different constructions have been put on
some of these words; but the context seems to
me to necessitate those before us. I quote, however, not from the original, but from an extract
in the Remarks on Paradise Lost by Richardson.

What the poet has to cultivate above all things
is love and truth;—what he has to avoid, like
poison, is the fleeting and the false. He will get
no good by proposing to be 'in earnest at the
moment.' His earnestness must be innate and
habitual; born with him, and felt to be his most
precious inheritance. 'I expect neither profit
or [2] general fame by my writings,' says Coleridge,
in the Preface to his Poems; 'and I consider
myself as having been amply repaid without
either. Poetry has been to me its "*own exceed-
ing great reward;*" it has soothed my afflictions;
it has multiplied and refined my enjoyments; it
has endeared solitude; and it has given me the
habit of wishing to discover the good and the
beautiful in all that meets and surrounds me.'[3]

'Poetry,' says Shelley, 'lifts the veil from
the hidden beauty of the world, *and makes*

---

[1] Not in comparison with science, but with rhetoric. See
Milton's tractate *On Education.*

[2] Hunt, 'nor.'

[3] Hunt inserts, 'Pickering's edition, p. 10;' but it is found in
all the good editions.

familiar objects be as if they were not familiar;
it reproduces all that it represents, and the
impersonations clothed in its Elysian light stand
thenceforward in the minds of those who have
once contemplated them, as memorials of that 5
gentle and exalted content which extends itself
over all thoughts and actions with which it
co-exists. The great secret of morals is love;
or a going out of our own nature, and an identi-
fication of ourselves with the beautiful which 10
exists in thought, action, or person, not our own.
A man, to be greatly good, must imagine intensely
and comprehensively; he must put himself in the
place of another, and of many others; the pains
and pleasures of his species must become his 15
own. The great instrument of moral good is
the[1] imagination; and poetry administers to the
effect by acting upon the cause.'[2]

I would not willingly say anything after perora-
tions like these; but as treatises on poetry may 10
chance to have auditors who think themselves
called upon to vindicate the superiority of what
is termed useful knowledge, it may be as well
to add, that if the poet may be allowed to pique
himself on any one thing more than another, 25
compared with those who undervalue him, it is
on that power of undervaluing nobody, and no
attainments different from his own, which is
given him by the very faculty of imagination

[1] Hunt omits 'the.'
[2] See my edition of the *Defense of Poetry*, 13 27–14 12; Hunt
inserts, ' Essays and Letters, vol. i, p. 16.'

they despise. ⌊The greater includes the less.
They do not see that their inability to compre-
hend him argues the smaller capacity.⌋ No man
recognizes the worth of utility more than the
poet; he only desires that the meaning of the
term may not come short of its greatness, and
exclude the noblest necessities of his fellow-
creatures.   He is quite as much pleased, for
instance, with the facilities for rapid conveyance
afforded him by the railroad, as the dullest con-
finer of its advantages to that single idea, or as
the greatest two-ideaed man who varies that single
idea with hugging himself on his 'buttons' or his
good dinner.   But he sees also the beauty of the
country through which he passes, of the towns, of
the heavens, of the steam-engine itself, thunder-
ing and fuming along like a magic horse, of the
affections that are carrying, perhaps, half the
passengers on their journey, nay, of those of the
great two-ideaed man; and, beyond all this, he
discerns the incalculable amount of good, and
knowledge, and refinement, and mutual consideration, which this wonderful invention is fitted to
circulate over the globe, perhaps to the displace-
ment of war itself, and certainly to the diffusion
of millions of enjoyments.

'And a button-maker, after all, invented it!'
cries our friend.

Pardon me — it was a nobleman.   A button-
maker may be a very excellent, and a very poetical
man too, and yet not have been the first man

visited by a sense of the gigantic powers of the
combination of water and fire. It was a nobleman who first thought of this most poetical bit of
science. It was a nobleman who first thought of
it — a captain who first tried it, — and a button- 5
maker who perfected it.[1] And he who put the
nobleman on such thoughts, was the great philos-
opher Bacon,[2] who said that poetry had 'something divine in it,'[3] and was necessary to the
satisfaction of the human mind. 10

[1] The Marquis of Worcester (1601–1667), Captain Savery (ca.
1650–1715), and Boulton (1728–1809), the business associate of
Watt, and, in some sense, co-inventor with him. It can hardly
be doubtful that Watt could not have introduced and perfected
his invention without the assistance of Boulton. See Smiles'
Lives of Boulton and Watt. Hunt's statement can, of course,
only be admitted in a rhetorical sense, and not at all as a precise
historical truth.

[2] Dircks says nothing of any indebtedness to Bacon in his
Life, Times, etc. of the Second Marquis of Worcester (London,
1865)

[3] From the *De Augment. Scient.* 2. 13 (ed. Spedding, Ellis,
and Heath, 1. 519): 'Divinitatis cujuspiam particeps videri
possit.' See *Adv. Learn.* 2. 4. 2.

NOTE ON THE DISTINCTION BETWEEN
IMAGINATION AND FANCY.

THE distinction between imagination and fancy, of which so much account has been made in English poetical criticism, was of course not originated by Leigh Hunt. So far as is known, Coleridge was the first English writer who effected a clear severance be- 5 tween the two, but he only elaborated upon a hint wnich he drew from Richter's Vorschule der Æsthetik (Brandl, Life of Coleridge, pp. 316–317). The theory is also found in one of Wordsworth's Prefaces, no doubt as a fruit of the discussions on poetry between 10 himself and Coleridge (see 79 16 ff., *infra*). Leigh Hunt, therefore, merely illustrates and confirms a view already current, as he, in turn, is quoted and enlarged upon by Ruskin in Vol. III. of Modern Painters ('Of Imagination Penetrative'). The passages from 15 Richter, Coleridge, and Wordsworth which establish the derivation of the theory are here appended. It will be noted that the 'fancy' of the English writers is by Richter termed 'Einbildungkraft,' while their 'imagination' is his 'Phantasie' oder 'Bildung- 20 kraft.'

Foot-notes are by the present editor, except as indicated.

I.

JEAN PAUL RICHTER.

[*Vorschule der Æsthetik*, Programm II, § 6 and 7.]

Einbildungkraft ist die Prose der Bildungkraft oder Phantasie. Sie ist nichts als eine potenzirte hellfarbigere Erinnerung,[1] welche auch die Thiere haben, weil sie träumen und weil sie fürchten. Ihre Bilder
5 sind nur zugeflogne Abblätterungen von der wirklichen Welt; Fieber, Nervenschwäche, Getränke können diese Bilder so verdicken und beleiben, dass sie aus der innern Welt in die äussere treten und darin zu Leibern erstarren.

10 Aber etwas höheres ist die Phantasie oder Bildungkraft, sie ist die Welt-Seele der Seele und der Elementargeist der übrigen Kräfte; darum kann eine grosse Phantasie zwar in die Richtungen einzelner Kräfte, z. B. des Witzes, des Scharfsinns u. s. w. abgegraben
15 und abgeleitet werden, aber keine dieser Kräfte lässet sich zur Phantasie erweitern. Wenn der Witz das spielende *Anagramm* der Natur ist, so ist die Phantasie das *Hieroglyphen-Alphabet* derselben, wovon sie mit wenigen Bildern ausgesprochen wird. Die Phantasie macht alle Theile zu Ganzen — statt dass die übrigen Kräfte und die Erfahrung aus dem Naturbuche nur Blätter reissen — und alle Welttheile zu Welten, sie totalisiret alles, auch das unendliche All; daher tritt in ihr Reich der poetische Optimismus, die Schön-
25 heit der Gestalten, die es bewohnen, und die Freiheit, womit in ihrem Aether die Wesen wie Sonnen gehen.

[1] See 80 16 ff.

Sie führt gleichsam das Absolute und das Unendliche
der Vernunft näher und anschaulicher vor den sterb-
lichen Menschen. Daher braucht sie so viel Zukunft
und so viel Vergangenheit, ihre beiden Schöpfung-
Ewigkeiten, weil keine andere Zeit unendlich oder zu   5
einem Ganzen werden kann ; nicht aus einem Zimmer
voll Luft, sondern erst aus der ganzen Höhe der Luft-
säule kann das Aetherblau eines Himmels geschaffen
werden.

II.

COLERIDGE.

[*Biographia Literaria*, chap. 4.]

Repeated meditations led me first to suspect — and   10
a more intimate analysis of the human faculties, their
appropriate marks, functions, and effects, matured my
conjecture into full conviction — that fancy and imagination were two distinct and widely different faculties,
instead of being, according to the general belief, either   15
two names with one meaning, or, at furthest, the lower
and higher degree of one and the same power. It is
not, I own, easy to conceive a more opposite translation of the Greek φαντασία than the Latin *imaginatio;*
but it is equally true that in all societies there exists   20
an instinct of growth, a certain collective, unconscious
good sense, working progressively to desynonymize
those words originally of the same meaning, which the
conflux of dialects had supplied to the more homo-
geneous languages, as the Greek and German, and   25
which the same cause, joined with accidents of translation from original works of different countries, occasion in mixed languages like our own. The first
and most important point to be proved is, that two

conceptions perfectly distinct are confused under one
and the same word, and — this done — to appropriate that word exclusively to one meaning, and the
synonyme, should there be one, to the other. But if
5 — as will be often the case in the arts and sciences
— no synonyme exists, we must either invent or
borrow a word. In the present instance the appro-
priation has[1] already begun, and been legitimated in
the derivative adjective : Milton had a highly *imagina-*
10 *tive*, Cowley a very *fanciful* mind. If, therefore, I
should succeed in establishing the actual existence of
two faculties generally different. the nomenclature
would be at once determined. To the faculty by
which I had characterized Milton, we should confine
15 the term *imagination;* while the other would be contradistinguished as *fancy.* Now were it once fully ascer-
tained that this division is no less grounded in nature
than that of *delirium* from *mania*, or Otway's

     Lutes, laurels, seas of milk, and ships of amber,[2]

20 from Shakespeare's

     What ! have his daughters brought him to this pass?[3]

or from the preceding apostrophe to the elements, the
theory of the fine arts, and of poetry in particular,
could not, I thought. but derive some additional and
25 important light. It would. in its immediate effects,
furnish a torch of guidance to the philosophical critic,
and ultimately to the poet himself. In energetic
minds truth soon changes by domestication into
power ; and, from directing in the discrimination and
30 appraisal of the product, becomes influencive in the

---

[1] First edition, 'had.'   [2] *Venice Preserved*, Act V.
[3] *King Lear* 3. 4. 66.

production. To admire on principle is the only way to imitate without loss of originality.

. . . There was a time, certainly, in which I took some little credit to myself in the belief that I had been the first of my countrymen who had pointed out 5 the diverse meaning of which the two terms were capable, and analyzed the faculties to which they should be appropriated. Mr. W. Taylor's recent volume of synonymes I have not yet seen ; but his specification of the terms in question [1] has been clearly 10 shown to be both insufficient and erroneous by Mr. Wordsworth, in the preface added to the late collection of his Lyrical Ballads, and other poems. The explanation which Mr. Wordsworth has himself given will be found to differ from mine chiefly, perhaps, as 15 our objects are different. It could scarcely indeed happen otherwise, from the advantage I have enjoyed of frequent conversation with him, on a subject to which a poem of his own first directed my attention, and my conclusions concerning which he had made 20 more lucid to myself by many happy instances drawn from the operation of natural objects on the mind. But it was Mr. Wordsworth's purpose to consider the influences of fancy and imagination as they are manifested in poetry, and from the different effects to con- 25 clude their diversity in kind ; while it is my object to investigate the seminal principle, and then from the kind to deduce the degree. My friend has drawn a masterly sketch of the branches, with their poetic fruitage. I wish to add the trunk, and even the 30 roots as far as they lift themselves above ground, and are visible to the naked eye of our common consciousness.

[1] *Cf. infra* 80 25–81 15.

The imagination then I consider either as primary or secondary. The primary imagination I hold to be the living power and prime agent of all human perception, and as a repetition in the finite mind of
5 the eternal act of creation in the infinite I AM. The secondary I consider as an echo of the former, co-existing with the conscious will, yet still as identical with the primary in the kind of its agency, and differing only in degree, and in the mode of its operation.
10 It dissolves, diffuses, dissipates, in order to re-create; or where this process is rendered impossible, yet still, at all events, it struggles to idealize and to unify. It it essentially vital, even as all objects (as objects) are essentially fixed and dead.
15 Fancy, on the contrary, has no other counters to play with but fixities and definites. The Fancy is indeed no other than a mode of memory[1] emancipated from the order of time and space; and blended with, and modified by, that empirical phenomenon of the
20 will, which we express by the word choice. But, equally with the ordinary memory, it must receive all its materials ready made from the law of association.

III.

WORDSWORTH.

[*Preface of* 1815–1845],

Let us come now to the consideration of the words Fancy and Imagination, as employed in the classifica-
25 tion of the following poems. 'A man,' says an intelligent author, 'has imagination in proportion as he can distinctly copy in idea the impressions of sense:

[1] *Cf.* 76 2.

it is the faculty which *images* within the mind the phe-
nomena of sensation. A man has fancy in proportion
as he can call up, connect, or associate, at pleasure,
those internal images (φαντάζειν is to cause to appear)
so as to complete ideal representations of absent ob- 5
jects. Imagination is the power of depicting, and
fancy of evoking and combining. The imagination is
formed by patient observation ; the fancy by a volun-
tary activity in shifting the scenery of the mind. The
more accurate the imagination, the more safely may a 10
painter, or a poet, undertake a delineation, or a description, without the presence of the objects to be
characterized. The more versatile the fancy, the more
original and striking will be the decorations produced.'
—*British Synonyms discriminated, by W. Taylor.* 15

Is not this as if a man should undertake to supply
an account of a building, and be so intent upon what
he had discovered of the foundation, as to conclude
his task without once looking up at the superstructure ?
Here, as in other instances throughout the volume, the 20
judicious Author's mind is enthralled by etymology ;
he takes up the original word as his guide and escort,
and too often does not perceive how soon he becomes
its prisoner, without liberty to tread in any path but
that to which it confines him. It is not easy to find 25
out how imagination, thus explained, differs from distinct remembrance of images ; or fancy from quick
and vivid recollection of them : each is nothing more
than a mode of memory. If the two words bear the
above meaning and no other, what term is left to 30
designate that faculty of which the poet is 'all compact' ;[1] he whose eye glances from earth to heaven,

[1] *Mid. N. D.* 5. 1. 8.

whose spiritual attributes body forth what his pen is
prompt in turning to shape ; or what is left to charac-
terize Fancy, as insinuating herself into the heart of
objects with creative activity?   Imagination, in the
5 sense of the word as giving title to a class of the
following poems, has no reference to images that are
merely a faithful copy, existing in the mind, of absent
external objects ; but is a word of higher import,
denoting operations of the mind upon those objects
10 and processes of creation or of composition, governed
by certain fixed laws. I proceed to illustrate my
meaning by instances.   A parrot *hangs* from the wires
of his cage by his beak or by his claws ; or a monkey
from the bough of a tree by his paws or his tail. Each
15 creature does so literally and actually. In the first
Eclogue of Virgil, the shepherd, thinking of the time
when he is to take leave of his farm, thus addresses
his goats : —

> Non ego vos posthac viridi projectus in antro
20 > Dumosa *pendere* procul de rupe videbo.

> —————— half way down
> *Hangs* one who gathers samphire,[1]

is the well-known expression of Shakespeare, delineat-
ing an ordinary image upon the cliffs of Dover.   In
25 these two instances is a slight exertion of the faculty
which I denominate imagination, in the use of one
word : neither the goats nor the samphire-gatherer do
literally hang, as does the parrot or the monkey ; but,
presenting to the senses something of such an appear-
30 ance, the mind in its activity, for its own gratification,
contemplates them as hanging.

[1] *King Lear* 4. 6. 14–15; 'who' for 'that.'

As when far off at sea a fleet descried
Hangs[1] in the clouds, by equinoctial winds
Close sailing from Bengala, or the isles
Of Ternate or Tidore, whence merchants bring
Their spicy drugs ; they on the trading flood,   5
Through the wide Ethiopian to the Cape,
Ply stemming nightly toward the pole ; so seemed
Far off the flying Fiend.[2]

Here is the full strength of the imagination involved
in the word *hangs*, and exerted upon the whole image: 10
First, the fleet, an aggregate of many ships, is represented as one mighty person, whose track, we know
and feel, is upon the waters ; but, taking advantage of
its appearance to the senses, the Poet dares to repre-
sent it as *hanging in the clouds*, both for the gratifica- 15
tion of the mind in contemplating the image itself, and
in reference to the motion and appearance of the
sublime objects to which it is compared.

From impressions of sight we will pass to those of
sound ; which, as they must necessarily be of a less 20
definite character, shall be selected from these volumes:

Over his own sweet voice the Stock-dove *broods* ;[3]

of the same bird,

His voice was *buried* among trees,
Yet to be come at by the breeze.[4]   25

O, Cuckoo! shall I call thee *Bird*,
Or but a wandering *Voice!*[5]

---

[1] *Cf. supra*, 12 1.
[2] *P. L.* 2. 636-643.
[3] Wordsworth, *Independence and Resolution.*
[4] Wordsworth, ' *O Nightingale! thou surely art.*'
[5] Wordsworth, *To the Cuckoo.*

The stock-dove is said to *coo*, a sound well imitating the note of the bird ; but, by the intervention of the metaphor *broods*, the affections are called in by the imagination to assist in marking the manner in which
5 the bird reiterates and prolongs her soft note, as if herself delighting to listen to it, and participating of a still and quiet satisfaction, like that which may be supposed inseparable from the continuous process of incubation. ' His voice was buried among the trees,'
10 a metaphor expressing the love of *seclusion* by which this bird is marked ; and characterizing its note as not partaking of the shrill and the piercing, and therefore more easily deadened by the intervening shade ; yet a note so peculiar and withal so pleasing, that the
15 breeze, gifted with that love of the sound which the poet feels, penetrates the shades in which it is entombed, and conveys it to the ear of the listener.

> Shall I call thee Bird,
> Or but a wandering Voice?

20 This concise interrogation characterizes the seeming ubiquity of the voice of the cuckoo, and dispossesses the creature almost of a corporeal existence ; the Imagination being tempted to this exertion of her power by a consciousness in the memory that the
25 cuckoo is almost perpetually heard throughout the season of spring, but seldom becomes an object of sight.

Thus far of images independent of each other and immediately endowed by the mind with properties that
30 do not inhere in them, upon an incitement from properties and qualities the existence of which is inherent and obvious. These processes of imagination are carried on either by conferring additional properties

upon an object, or abstracting from it some of those
which it actually possesses, and thus enabling it to re-
act upon the mind which hath performed the process,
like a new existence.

I pass from the Imagination acting upon an indi- 5
vidual image to a consideration of the same faculty
employed upon images in a conjunction by which they
modify each other. The reader has already had a
fine instance before him in the passage quoted from
Virgil, where the apparently perilous situation of the 10
goat, hanging upon the shaggy precipice, is contrasted
with that of the shepherd contemplating it from the
seclusion of the cavern in which he lies stretched at
ease and in security. Take these images separately,
and how unaffecting the picture compared with that 15
produced by their being thus connected with and
opposed to, each other !

> As a huge stone is sometimes seen to lie
> Couched on the bald top of an eminence,
> Wonder to all who do the same espy   20
> By what means it could thither come, and whence,
> So that it seems a thing endued with sense,
> Like a sea-beast crawled forth, which on a shelf
> Of rock or sand reposeth, there to sun himself.

> Such seemed this Man ; not all alive or dead   25
> Nor all asleep, in his extreme old age.

> .   .   .   .

> Motionless as a cloud the old Man stood,
> That heareth not the loud winds when they call,
> And moveth altogether if it move at all.[1]

In these images, the conferring, the abstracting, and 30
the modifying powers of the Imagination, immediately

---

[1] Wordsworth's *Resolution and Independence;* but with slight
variations from the received text of the poem.

and mediately acting, are all brought into conjunction.
The stone is endowed with something of the power of
life to approximate it to the sea-beast ; and the sea-
beast stripped of some of its vital qualities to assimi-
5 late it to the stone ; which intermediate image is thus
treated for the purpose of bringing the original image,
that of the stone, to a nearer resemblance to the
figure and condition of the aged man ; who is divested
of so much of the indications of life and motion as to
10 bring him to the point where the two objects unite
and coalesce in just comparison. After what has
been said, the image of the cloud need not be com-
mented upon.

Thus far of an endowing or modifying power : but
15 the Imagination also shapes and *creates;* and how?
By innumerable processes : and in none does it more
delight than in that of consolidating numbers into
unity, and dissolving and separating unity into number,   alternations proceeding from, and governed by,
20 a sublime consciousness of the soul in her own mighty
and almost divine powers. Recur to the passage already cited from Milton. When the compact fleet,
as one person, has been introduced 'Sailing from
Bengala.' 'They,' *i.e.* the 'merchants,' representing
25 the fleet, resolved into a multitude of ships, 'ply'
their voyage towards the extremities of the earth :
' So ' (referring to the word ' As ' in the commencement)
'seemed the flying Fiend ;' the image of his person
acting to recombine the multitude of ships into one
30 body, — the point from which the comparison set out.
' So seemed,' and to whom seemed ? To the heavenly
Muse who dictates the poem, to the eye of the poet's
mind, and to that of the reader, present at one moment in the wide Ethiopian, and the next in the

solitudes, then first broken in upon, of the infernal
regions !

Modo me Thebis, modo ponit Athenis.[1]

Here again this mighty poet, speaking of the Messiah
going forth to expel from heaven the rebellious angels, 5

> Attended by ten thousand thousand Saints,
> He onward came : far off his coming shone, — [2]

the retinue of saints, and the Person of the Messiah
himself, lost almost and merged in the splendor of
that indefinite abstraction, 'His coming !' 10
As I do not mean here to treat this subject further
than to throw some light upon the present volumes,
and especially upon one division of them, I shall
spare myself and the reader the trouble of considering the Imagination as it deals with thoughts and 15
sentiments, as it regulates the composition of characters and determines the course of actions : I will not
consider it (more than I have already done by impli-
cation) as that power which, in the language of one
of my most esteemed friends, 'draws all things to one ; 20
which makes things animate or inanimate, beings with
their attributes, subjects with their accessories, take
one color and serve to one effect.'[3] The grand store-
houses of enthusiastic and meditative Imagination, of
poetical, as contradistinguished from human and dra- 25
matic Imagination, are the prophetic and lyrical parts
of the Holy Scriptures, and the works of Milton ; to
which I cannot forbear to add those of Spenser. I
select these writers in preference to those of ancient
Greece and Rome, because the anthropomorphitism 30

---

[1] Horace, *Epist.* 2. 1. 213. [2] *P. L.* 6. 767-768.
[3] Charles Lamb upon the genius of Hogarth. (Wordsworth's note.)

of the Pagan religion subjected the minds of the
greatest poets in those countries too much to the
bondage of definite form ; from which the Hebrews
were preserved by their abhorrence of idolatry. This
5 abhorrence was almost as strong in our great epic
Poet, both from circumstances of his life, and from
the constitution of his mind However imbued the
surface might be with classical literature, he was a
Hebrew in soul ; and all things tended in him towards
10 the sublime. Spenser, of a gentler nature, maintained
his freedom by aid of his allegorical spirit, at one time
inciting him to create persons out of abstractions ; and,
at another, by a superior effort of genius, to give the
universality and permanence of abstractions to his
15 human beings, by means of attributes and emblems
that belong to the highest moral truths and the purest
sensations, — of which his character of Una is a glorious example. Of the human and dramatic Imagination the works of Shakespeare are an inexhaustible
20 source.

> I tax not you, ye elements, with unkindness,
> I never gave you kingdoms, call'd you daughters ! [1]

And if, bearing in mind the many poets distinguished
by this prime quality, whose names I omit to mention;
25 yet justified by recollection of the insults which the
ignorant, the incapable and the presumptuous, have
heaped upon these and my other writings, I may be
permitted to anticipate the judgment of posterity upon
myself, I shall declare (censurable, I grant, if the
30 notoriety of the fact above stated does not justify me)
that I have given in these unfavorable times, evidence

[1] *King Lear* 3. 2. 14-15; with substitution of 'ye' for 'you,'
'kingdoms' for 'kingdom,' and 'daughters' for 'children.'

of exertions of this faculty upon its worthiest objects, the external universe, the moral and religious senti- ments of Man, his natural affections, and his acquired passions ; which have the same ennobling tendency as the productions of men, in this kind, worthy to be 5 holden in undying remembrance.

To the mode in which Fancy has already been char- acterized as the power of evoking and combining, or, as my friend Mr. Coleridge has styled it, 'the aggrega- tive and associative power,' my objection is only that 10 the definition is too general. To aggregate and to associate, to evoke and to combine, belong as well to the Imagination as to the Fancy ; but either the materials evoked and combined are different : or they are brought together under a different law, and for a 15 different purpose. Fancy does not require that the materials which she makes use of should be suscep- tible of change in their constitution, from her touch ; and, where they admit of modification, it is enough for her purpose if it be slight, limited, and evanescent. 20 Directly the reverse of these are the desires and demands of the Imagination. She recoils from every- thing but the plastic, the pliant, and the indefinite. She leaves it to Fancy to describe Queen Mab as coming, 25

In shape no bigger than an agate-stone
On the fore-finger of an alderman.[1]

Having to speak of stature, she does not tell you that her gigantic Angel was as tall as Pompey's Pillar : much less that he was twelve cubits, or twelve hundred 30 cubits high ; or that his dimensions equalled those of Teneriffe or Atlas : — because these, and if they were

[1] *Rom. and Jul.* I. 4. 55–56; *cf. supra*, 35 5 ff.

a million times as high it would be the same, are
bounded : The expression is, ' His stature reached the
sky!'[1] the illimitable firmament !—When the Imagination frames a comparison, if it does not strike on the
first presentation, a sense of the truth of the likeness,
from the moment that it is perceived, grows—and
continues to grow—upon the mind ; the resemblance
depending less upon outline of form and feature, than
upon expression and effect ; less upon casual and out-
standing, than upon inherent and internal, properties :
moreover, the images invariably modify each other. —
The law under which the processes of Fancy are
carried on is as capricious as the accidents of things,
and the effects are surprising, playful, ludicrous, amus-
ing, tender, or pathetic, as the objects happen to be
appositely produced or fortunately combined. Fancy
depends upon the rapidity and profusion with which
she scatters her thoughts and images ; trusting that
their number, and the felicity with which they are
linked together, will make amends for the want of individual value : or she prides herself upon the curious
subtilty and the successful elaboration with which she
can detect their lurking affinities. If she can win you
over to her purpose, and impart to you her feelings,
she cares not how unstable or transitory may be her
influence, knowing that it will not be out of her power
to resume it upon an apt occasion. But the Imagination is conscious of an indestructible dominion ; — the
Soul may fall away from it, not being able to sustain
its grandeur ; but, if once felt and acknowledged, by
no act of any other faculty of the mind can it be re-
laxed, impaired, or diminished. — Fancy is given to

[1] P. L. 4. 988.

quicken and to beguile the temporal part of our nature,
Imagination to incite and to support the eternal. ——
Yet is it not the less true that Fancy, as she is an
active, is also, under her own laws and in her own
spirit, a creative faculty. In what manner Fancy am-   5
bitiously aims at a rivalship with Imagination, and
Imagination stoops to work with materials of Fancy,
might be illustrated from the compositions of all elo-
quent writers, whether in prose or verse ; and chiefly
from those of our own country.   Scarcely a page of 10
the impassioned parts of Bishop Taylor's Works can
be opened that shall not afford examples. — Referring
the Reader to those inestimable volumes, I will content myself with placing a conceit (ascribed to Lord
Chesterfield) in contrast with a passage from the 15
Paradise Lost:——

> The dews of the evening most carefully shun,
> They are the[1] tears of the sky for the loss of the sun.[2]

After the transgression of Adam, Milton, with other
appearances of sympathizing Nature, thus marks the 20
immediate consequence,

> Sky lowered, and, muttering thunder, some sad drops
> Wept at completion[3] of the mortal sin.[4]

The associating link is the same in each instance:
Dew and rain, not distinguishable from the liquid sub- 25
stance of tears, are employed as indications of sorrow.
A flash of surprise is the effect in the former case; a
flash of surprise, and nothing more ; for the nature of

[1] Properly 'those,' for 'they are the.'
[2] Chesterfield, *Advice to a Lady in Autumn*.
[3] Rather, 'completing.'
[4] *P. L.* 9. 1002–1003.

things does not sustain the combination.   In the latter, the effects from the act, of which there is this
immediate consequence and visible sign, are so mo-
mentous, that the mind acknowledges the justice and
5 reasonableness of the sympathy in nature so manifested ; and the sky weeps drops of water as if with
human eyes, as ' Earth had before trembled from her
entrails, and Nature given a second groan.' [1]

Finally, I will refer to Cotton's Ode upon Winter,
10 an admirable composition, though stained with some
peculiarities of the age in which he lived, for a general illustration of the characteristics of Fancy.   The
middle part of this ode contains a most lively description of the entrance of Winter, with his retinue, as
15 ' A palsied king,' and yet a military monarch, — ad-
vancing for conquest with his army; the several bodies
of which, and their arms and equipments, are described with a rapidity of detail, and a profusion of
fanciful comparisons, which indicate on the part of the
20 poet extreme activity of intellect, and a correspondent
hurry of delightful feeling.   Winter retires from the
foe into his fortress, where

——— a magazine
Of sovereign juice is cellared in ;
25   Liquor that will the siege maintain
Should Phœbus ne'er return again.

Though myself a water-drinker, I cannot resist the
pleasure of transcribing what follows, as an instance
still more happy of Fancy employed in the treatment
30 of feeling than, in its preceding passages, the Poem
supplies of her management of forms.

[1] Adapted from *P. L.* 9. 1000–1001.

'Tis that, that gives the poet rage,
And thaws the gelly'd [1] blood of age ;
Matures the young, restores the old,
And makes the fainting coward bold.

It lays the careful head to rest,   5
Calms palpitations in the breast,
Renders our lives' misfortune sweet;

.   .   .   .

Then let the chill Sirocco blow,
And gird us round with hills of snow,
Or else go whistle to the shore,   10
And make the hollow mountains roar,

Whilst we together jovial sit
Careless, and crowned with mirth and wit,
Where, though bleak winds confine us home,
Our fancies round the world shall roam.   15

We'll think of all the friends we know,
And drink to all worth drinking to;
When having drunk all thine and mine,
We rather shall want healths than wine.

But where friends fail us, we'll supply   20
Our friendships with our charity;
Men that remote in sorrows live,
Shall by our lusty brimmers thrive.

We'll drink the wanting into wealth,
And those that languish into health,   25
The afflicted into joy, the opprest
Into security and rest.

The worthy in disgrace shall find
Favor return again more kind,
And in restraint who stifled lie,   30
Shall taste the air of liberty.

     [1] Qu. 'gelid,' or 'jellied'?

The brave shall triumph in success,
The lovers shall have mistresses,
Poor unregarded Virtue, praise,
And the neglected Poet, bays.

5   Thus shall our healths do others good,
Whilst we ourselves do all we would;
For, freed from envy and from care,
What would we be but what we are?

INDEX OF PROPER NAMES.

ANNOUNCEMENTS

BOOKS ON HIGHER ENGLISH

Edited by ALBERT S. COOK

Professor of the English Language and Literature in Yale University

---

ADDISON'S CRITICISMS ON PARADISE LOST. 12mo, cloth, xxiv + 200 pages, $1.00.

ASSER'S LIFE OF KING ALFRED. Translated with Notes from the text of Stevenson's edition. 12mo, cloth, 83 pages, 50 cents.

BACON'S ADVANCEMENT OF LEARNING, Book I. 12mo, cloth, lvii + 145 pages, 75 cents.

CARDINAL NEWMAN'S ESSAY ON POETRY. With reference to Aristotle's Poetics. 8vo, flexible cloth, x + 36 pages, 30 cents.

LEIGH HUNT'S ANSWER TO THE QUESTION "WHAT IS POETRY?" Including remarks on Versification. 12mo, cloth, vi + 98 pages, 50 cents.

SHELLEY'S DEFENSE OF POETRY. 12mo, cloth, xxvi + 86 pages, 50 cents.

SIDNEY'S DEFENSE OF POESY. 12mo, cloth, xlv + 103 pages, 65 cents

THE ART OF POETRY. The Poetical Treatises of Horace, Vida, Boileau, with the translations by Howes, Pitt, and Soame. 12mo, cloth, lviii + 303 pages, $1.12.

TENNYSON'S THE PRINCESS. 16mo, semiflexible cloth, xlvi + 187 pages, 30 cents.

EDMUND CLARENCE STEDMAN, Author of "Victorian Poets," "Poets of America," "The Nature and Elements of Poetry," etc.

More than once of late, when asked to name for some friend or correspondent a course of reading upon the spirit and structure of poetry, I have at once recommended Professor Albert S. Cook's series, and have been grateful to him for his admirable labors. He could have made no better choice of treatises to edit: Sidney, Shelley, Addison, Hunt, and Newman have had no better editor — so far as their exquisite essays upon the divine art are concerned. Professor Cook's notes are the fruit of sympathetic taste and liberal scholarship. The books, in fact, are models as handbooks, upon an ideal subject, designed for practical use.

GINN AND COMPANY Publishers

RECENT BOOKS IN LITERATURE

SCHILLER

By EUGEN KÜHNEMANN, Professor of Philosophy in the University of Breslau, Germany. Translated by KATHARINE ROYCE. Two volumes, 8vo, cloth, 844 pages, with frontispiece, $3.00.

THERE is no study in English which so adequately treats the literary, the critical, the philosophical, the æsthetic, and the ethical aspects of Schiller's personality and life work as Professor Kühnemann's " Life of Schiller." The author discusses at length the influences which determined Schiller's personal and artistic development from his youth to the maturity of his powers, his permanent literary significance, and his relation to the dramatic poetry of his predecessors and successors.

SOCIAL FORCES IN MODERN LITERATURE

By PHILO M. BUCK, JR., Professor of Rhetoric in the University of Nebraska. 12mo, cloth, 254 pages, $1.00.

THIS study of European literature of the past century traces the gradual rise of the interest of pure literature in the mutual relation of man and society, and discusses in detail the various answers essayed by six leading writers — Montesquieu, Rousseau, Lessing, Goethe, Wordsworth, and Shelley. The book is excellently adapted to classes in comparative literature and will be found of interest to the general reader.

WORDSWORTH—POET OF NATURE AND POET OF MAN

By E. HERSHEY SNEATH, Lecturer on Ethics and Religious Education in Yale University. 8vo, cloth, 320 pages, $2.00.

THE author traces in detail the history of Wordsworth's mental and spiritual development as a poet, showing the influence upon him of heredity and physical and social environment. The volume forms a complete statement of Wordsworth's poetic and philosophic creed.

ARISTOTLE ON THE ART OF POETRY

Translated and adapted by LANE COOPER, Assistant Professor of English in Cornell University. 12mo, cloth, xxix + 101 pages, 80 cents.

THIS amplified version of the " Poetics " aims to make this important treatise as intelligible as may be for a first reading by students of modern literatures. The sequence of ideas is indicated by a running marginal gloss and difficulties are removed through interpolated comments, particularly additional examples from Shakespeare, Milton, and other familiar sources.

47

GINN AND COMPANY Publishers

ENGLISH POETRY (1170–1892)

Selected by JOHN MATTHEWS MANLY, Professor and Head of the Department of English in The University of Chicago

4to, cloth, xxviii + 580 pages, $1.50

NO other single volume equal in range and price to Manly's "English Poetry" has yet been placed before the teaching public. Professor Manly has brought together not merely as many poems as a teacher could expect his class to read in a course on English literature, but practically all from which any teacher choosing those most in harmony with his own taste and best suited to the special needs of his students would wish to select. The book includes some fifty thousand lines of poetry, ranging in date from the beginning of the Middle-English period to the death of Tennyson. Two principles have determined the choice of the poems, — their intrinsic worth and beauty, and their special significance in the history of English literature. The selections are unencumbered by notes, and historical and critical information has largely been omitted. Explanatory footnotes make clear the extracts from Middle or Early Modern English.

ENGLISH PROSE (1137–1890)

By JOHN MATTHEWS MANLY, Professor and Head of the Department of English in The University of Chicago

4to, cloth, xix + 544 pages, $1.50

THIS book is a companion volume to Manly's "English Poetry," and, like it, is intended primarily for use in a general survey of English literature. It contains so much material, however, that it will be found well adapted also for use in many special courses. The aim in both of these books has been to afford the teacher an opportunity to make his own selection for class use. Long selections (usually whole pieces) showing sustained power and control of organic structure have been chosen in preference to short bits of writing, however brilliant.

GINN AND COMPANY PUBLISHERS

THE ELEMENTS OF ENGLISH VERSIFICATION

By James Wilson Bright, Professor of English Literature in the Johns Hopkins University, and Raymond D. Miller, Instructor in English in the University of Missouri

12mo, cloth, xii + 166 pages, 80 cents

As the title indicates, "The Elements of English Versification" deals exclusively with the more external side of poetry, — its metrical form. Part One treats of the individual verse: it shows the nature of rhythm, meter, melody, harmony; enumerates and illustrates the various meters; defines tone color and the different kinds of rime; and concludes with an important chapter on the scansion of verse. Part Two is concerned with the grouping of verses into paragraphs, stanzas, and complete poems. An exhaustive index of topics and authors increases the value of the book as a manual of reference.

The subject is presented in a brief, impersonal style, illuminated at every point by varied and unhackneyed illustration. The treatment is broad and entirely free from controversial matter.

SHAKSPERE'S VERSIFICATION

By George H. Browne, of The Browne and Nichols School, Cambridge, Mass.

12mo, paper, 34 pages, interleaved, 25 cents

This treatise includes notes on "Shakspere's Versification," with an appendix on the verse tests and a short descriptive bibliography.

In speaking of the book, Professor Dowden says: "It deserves to be pointed out to students of this subject as an excellent introduction to the study of Shakespeare's verse."

PRIMER OF ENGLISH VERSE

By Hiram Corson, Emeritus Professor of English Literature in Cornell University

12mo, cloth, 232 pages, $1.00

The leading purpose of this volume is to introduce the student to the æsthetic and organic character of English verse. Tennyson's stanzas, the Spenserian stanzas, sonnets, and blank verse are specially treated.

GINN AND COMPANY Publishers